Facing the Darkness

Against the Darkness 1

H. L. Wegley

Suspense

Cover Design: Samantha Fury
http://www.furycoverdesign.com/

Cover Font: Jason Walcott
http://www.onlinewebfonts.com

Also available in ebook publication

Dedication

America is emerging from a two-year struggle against money and power mongers trying to take advantage of our people during a pandemic. Doctors were pressured to violate their oaths or, in many cases, were deceived into doing so without realizing it.

I am dedicating *Facing the Darkness* to those medical professionals who cared enough about their patients and their practice of medicine to seek out the truth in a domain of deception and who, when bureaucrats interfered and threatened, treated their patients to the best of their ability regardless of the consequences. May God bless you. America needs more men and women with your integrity.

Contents

You shall not be afraid of the terror by night, nor of the arrow that flies by day, nor of the pestilence that walks in darkness ...
Psalm 91:5,6 (NKJV)

Chapter 1

6:00 a.m., January 2, Wuhan, China

One cannot destroy a major research project at the Wuhan Institute of Virology, steal all the research results, and expect to live a long life. But twenty-nine-year-old Dr. Meiling Chen, MD, Ph.D., was a woman who had always exceeded expectations.

Under cover of darkness, Meiling left her apartment near East Lake, a little north of the Wuhan lab. As she traversed a section of the walkway that compassed the lake, footsteps in the distance behind her sent tingling chills up the back of her neck.

Her fear did not come from anything she had done but from what she was about to do.

After the footsteps faded, Meiling stopped beside the lake. She removed the battery from her cell phone and threw both the cell and the battery into the dark water. That would hinder the twenty-four-hour surveillance conducted by the Chinese Communist Party, the CCP, but they had other less pervasive means of tracking her.

At some point, CCP agents or the People's Liberation Army, via the PLA military police, would come after Meiling to do much more than disappear her because treachery was the greatest sin against the party, a sin punished by torture and death.

But what would grate the most on the pride of the CCP is that they had, for the first time, offered a post-doctoral fellowship to a virologist, an outsider from the Hong Kong School of Medicine, and she had, as the Americans say, ripped them off and escaped before they could do the same with her breakthrough in molecular virology.

Meiling, you've got to stop thinking about such things. Stay focused.

The voice inside was right. She needed to concentrate on one thing now, getting to the Wuhan terminal and catching her flight to Hong Kong.

Her nearly seven-hour, one-stop flight from Wuhan to Hong Kong would depart at 8:00 a.m., only two hours from now. By taking the 6:30 a.m. train to the airport, Meiling would minimize her time in the Wuhan terminal, a place the military police would certainly check if they became suspicious about her leaving Wuhan.

But hopefully, her vacation diversion, an apparent visit with her family in Hong Kong, would not trigger any immediate alarms. If it did not, that would delay efforts to track her down, especially without a cell phone to ping.

She would arrive in Hong Kong at 2:45 p.m. and should be in the Hong Kong University Medical School (HKUMed) lab by four o'clock this afternoon.

That would give Meiling nearly twenty-four hours in Hong Kong before flying to San Francisco. It was more than enough time to complete her data transfer from Wuhan to the storage media she had left at the HKUMed lab. From there, she would destroy all the RNA Virus Project's data in the Wuhan lab, and then—that was where her escape plan became both murky and menacing.

Since she had not made her international flight reservations yet, Meiling probably could not catch a flight to San Francisco before tomorrow afternoon. By then, her treachery would likely be discovered, and military police would be chasing her. The first place they would look would be the Hong Kong air terminal. And they would concentrate on Terminal 2, the terminal used for international flights.

The most perplexing question was, how could she keep her purchase of a ticket to the U.S. from being discovered before the flight departed? The CCP surveilled everyone in China, especially scientists doing sensitive research. She must solve this problem, or her escape attempt would die in Hong Kong and possibly Meiling with it.

The greatest dangers for her in Hong Kong would be first at the HKUMed lab tonight, when she would be using the Internet, and then at the airport tomorrow, when a ticket would tell the CCP the gate where Meiling would be waiting and when she would be there.

Maybe Pastor Lin at her old church in Hong Kong could help her negotiate the airport. Rumors said that he had helped others safely escape China.

* * *

Meiling's flight to Hong Kong was uneventful. Maybe her vacation-in-Hong-Kong ruse was working. And her flight arriving forty-five minutes late was a blessing in disguise. It would be dark when she arrived at the university, making it more likely that no one would see her enter the lab.

By the time she got a cab and rode to a neighborhood within walking distance of the university, it was a little after four o'clock.

Since she had tossed her old cell into the lake in Wuhan, Meiling stopped at a cell phone store about two kilometers from HKU and bought a burner phone. It had been almost twelve hours since she had eaten anything, so she stopped at the McDonald's next to the cell phone shop for a fast-food dinner.

As she walked to HKUMed, a low cloud deck moved in shortly before sunset. The dark twilight allowed her to approach the medical lab without being recognized. And on a Saturday evening, there was a good chance no one would be around to see her enter the lab.

So far, her escape had gone so well that perhaps God had heard and answered her prayers. But Meiling had many reasons to doubt His favor on one who followed Jesus in such a meandering way.

Depart from me. I never knew you.

Were those words written for hypocrites like Meiling Chen? The answer to that question would have to wait a while, and she would need a mature Jesus follower to provide the answer.

At 6:30 p.m., Meiling trotted up the steps to the HKU Clinical Research Centre and scurried across the large circular walkway to the entrance.

The Research Centre towering over her used to seem like home, but as of today, Meiling Chen had no home. She prayed that she would live long enough to find a new home somewhere in America. But that would be primarily determined by how carefully she performed her task in the lab.

By using the stairwell instead of the elevator, she reached the lab floor without encountering anyone.

At 7:00 p.m., Meiling stood outside the lab door listening for the sounds of people working. When she heard nothing, she cracked the door and peered inside. She could see to the corner by the lockers. Around the corner was the work area. No sounds came from it, so she would assume no one was working there.

She opened her locker and pulled three 512GB SD cards from a small box where she kept her storage media.

Meiling took a deep breath and peeked around the corner.

No one.

The lab administrator kept three state-of-the-art laptops for use by researchers in this section of the lab. She inserted her three SD cards, one into each of the three laptops.

5

From this point until she logged out, Meiling could be discovered and quickly tracked to her location in Hong Kong.

This will impact more lives than just mine. Please, God, do not let them detect me before I am finished.

On each laptop, she opened a browser and navigated to the Dubya IV research web server in Wuhan. Meiling logged in through the firewall, using an administrator's account that she had acquired by flirting with a young network administrator while she looked over his shoulder. Finally, she logged in to her personal research account.

Meiling navigated to the directories she wanted to download and started three parallel downloads that would decrypt and retrieve all her important research data.

The HKU medical research lab had a fast server, but it would still take at least an hour to download her data. And at this juncture, she was extremely vulnerable to detection. However, backups were done on Sunday nights, so unless some system administrator or network analyst in Wuhan had worked late this Saturday night and discovered the data transfer, she should complete the download without detection.

A single footstep sounded in the hallway.

Meiling froze.

The footstep morphed into several footsteps, now accompanied by muffled voices in the hall outside the lab door.

You must hide, Meiling.

Whether the message came as a voice or a thought, she did not know. But she could not risk being caught by CCP agents or the PLA's military police.

And I cannot leave any clues as to what the three laptops are doing.

There was one option that took only seconds to implement. She pressed Windows-L on each laptop, locking them but allowing the transfers to continue. Anyone not having the PINs for the lab computers would not be able to see what was happening on these three laptops.

But what about her? Was there any place in the long, narrow lab to stuff a five-foot-four, one-hundred-fifteen-pound woman?

Maybe.

Two men's voices had grown deep, gruff, and loud. They did not sound like college students.

"Check out Dr. Chen's lab. If she is not there, we will move on to the airport."

The search for Dr. Meiling Chen had begun. Meiling's pulse shifted into a higher gear.

Evidently, someone at Wuhan thought her leaving for Hong Kong was suspicious. That must have triggered a search by these agents looking for her. In a few more seconds, they could enter the lab section where she was working.

The sounds of locker doors opening and closing meant the men searching the lockers were now in the lab and approaching the corner that would allow them to peer into her part of the lab.

Should she pretend to be working on an HKUMed project and hope they would accept her story?

No. These men were skilled at interrogation. There was no hope of talking her way out of the situation if they found her.

Her heart pounded against her sternum as if it were attempting suicide. That would be better than falling into the clutches of the angry CCP or the murderous PLA.

You must hide, Meiling.

The message came again pleading, urgent.

She scanned the modular furniture in the long, narrow lab. It consisted of filing cabinets rolled under the workbenches that lined the two long walls of the medical lab.

Meiling prayed that while she was away at Wuhan, the lab manager had not gotten the approval to install the upgrade to the air-conditioning system. If he had not, there should still be an empty, framed-in hole in the wall behind one of the filing cabinets.

But which one?

She had one chance to guess the correct cabinet, but she was out of time. Meiling chose the filing cabinet nearest to her and rolled it out into the room.

Underneath the workbench, darkness hid the depth of a framed-in hole in the wall.

She had guessed correctly, but would she fit in the hole?

Meiling slung her purse into the opening and slid in feet-first. She pushed her body farther into the dark hole, feeling her way with her feet.

Before she moved out of reach, she hooked her fingers under the back of the cabinet and rolled it toward her.

Had the men rounded the corner? Did they see her? Were they mocking her vain effort to hide? Her only chance was to continue snaking her body into the hole.

She slid to her waist inside the framed hole while her feet extended back into who knew what. She tried to force from her mind thoughts of her phobias and fears about bats and bugs.

Once she was in far enough, Meiling pulled the rolling file cabinet back into place. It should hide her completely unless the men looked behind the cabinet.

The voices now came from inside the room, somewhere near her.

Meiling struggled to silence her breathing, but the mustiness in the dark hole made her nose itch and burn.

She was going to sneeze.

To stifle it, she laid the side of her finger above her upper lip and then pressed as hard as she could on a nerve that aided the urge to sneeze.

The sneeze came, but it was muted.

The men had been talking. Maybe they had not heard.

But what were they saying?

"What are these laptops doing? Lights are blinking at an incredible rate. But they're locked."

She choked on the musty odor. The sides of the air-duct hole seemed to press in on her as if they were crushing her chest. She could not breathe.

Technically she was breathing because air was going in and out of her lungs, but it was not helping. It was not enough.

Claustrophobia began its relentless attack, and it stole more of her sanity with each inadequate breath.

She had to stifle her panic. But, like the sneeze, it came anyway.

"Do not bother with the laptops. Any lab worker might be using them," one of the gruff voices said. "See if there are any signs she was here and look for any clues as to what she was doing."

Something bumped the rolling file hiding her.

She grabbed the two back wheels and jammed her hands between the castors and their mounts to stop any attempt to move the cabinet.

Maybe the man would think this cabinet was attached to the workbenches or to the wall.

Heavy breathing sounded hardly two feet in front of her face.

An unseen force pulled on the file cabinet.

Her fingers screamed their complaint at being pinched between the wheels and the mounting brackets.

She bit her tongue to stop her budding cry.

Blood trickled down one of her hands, but with her fingers as the brakes, the cabinet did not roll.

The man gave up his attempt. "There is no place for anyone to hide in here."

"While we are here, she could be boarding a plane for the United States," the other man said.

Were they leaving?

"But we must not miss her if she is here. Take another look around for a closet or something else she could crawl into."

"But there is no such place."

As the pain in her fingers subsided, her inadequate breaths and the cramped, confining space turned her breathing to panting.

She needed air, now!

Meiling pushed the rolling cabinet out into the room, lunged forward in an army crawl until she lay on the lab floor, and greedily sucked in the fresh air.

Only after she had filled her lungs several times did she realize the two men were gone.

She rose to her knees and waited until Dr. Meiling Chen was once again in control of her body and mind, and then she reached into the hole in the wall and retrieved her purse.

Meiling grabbed the edge of a workbench and pulled herself to her feet.

Thankfully, the laptops looked undisturbed, and the lights on their hard drives were still rapidly blinking.

She located the first aid kit on the lab wall and treated and bandaged her lacerated index finger.

Forty-five minutes later, all three downloads had finished, and Meiling had completely regained her composure.

Now for the coup de grace.

She changed to the root directory and erased the encryption key, rendering the entire RNA Virus project unreadable.

A system administrator would eventually try to restore the deleted data from a previous system backup. But the backups did not contain the encryption key. The key supposedly belonged to Meiling exclusively. But whether that was true or not, she did not know.

Regardless, they could not recover all the data defining her breakthrough. She had memorized that information, and not even threat of torture could pry it from her.

On each laptop, Meiling logged out from her account and then logged out from the Wuhan firewall account. She cleared the browser histories, pulled the SD cards out, and stuffed them in her purse. She would find a better hiding place for the SD cards later.

There were probably logs on the three laptops that she could purge to cover what she had done, but it was more important now to leave the university than to try to cover her tracks.

Since the men, either CCP agents or PLA police, had gone to the airport to find her, Meiling would need some way to navigate through the airport without giving herself away. And with China's pervasive surveillance system, buying a ticket would be telling those men when and at what gate to arrest her.

It was time to call Pastor Lin. Rumors said he had helped others in similar situations. Before she left for her fellowship at Wuhan, he had offered to help her if she ever needed to leave Hong Kong.

Meiling fished through her purse until she found the card on which she had written several phone numbers that she might need in an emergency.

Why was her old pastor's number at the bottom of the list? That conveyed a message about something Meiling had neglected for two years, something she did not want to think about now.

She punched in Pastor Lin's number.

"This is the Lin residence."

"Pastor Lin, this is Meiling Chen."

"Meiling, it is good to hear from you. I was concerned about you after you told me you would be working among the wolves at Wuhan."

"Pastor, I am afraid the wolves are chasing me, and I need to leave—"

"Stop, Meiling. Come to my house. It is a more appropriate place to have this discussion. Even in Hong Kong, we never know who may be listening."

"Thank you. I will be there in about fifteen minutes if I can avoid ..."

"No, Meiling. You *will* be here in fifteen minutes, because I am praying for you."

It was almost nine o'clock when Meiling approached the door of Pastor Lin's home.

Before she left for Wuhan two years ago, the pastor had said he knew people who could help her if she ever needed to leave Hong Kong secretly. She prayed those people were still around.

Meiling raised her hand to knock, but she gasped when the door swung open, leaving her staring into a dark room.

A strong hand swept her into the darkness.

Someone shut the door behind her.

The lock clicked.

Chapter 2

January 2, 9:00 p.m., Pastor Lin's home, Hong Kong

After the door latch clicked, lights came on.

The pastor's arm had swept Meiling into his dark living room.

The pastor's wife, Lihua, stood smiling at Meiling.

Pastor Lin motioned toward a chair. "First, tell us about your time in Wuhan, then about your current situation. And do not worry, Meiling. We can help you."

"You once told me that you knew people who could help me."

He smiled. "I know myself and my wife, do I not?"

Meiling dropped her purse in the big chair and sat.

The pastor and Lihua pulled up small chairs in front of her.

"I was surprised that you accepted the fellowship. We prayed for you for those two years without knowing how you were faring in Satan's lair. We know it is much different there than in Hong Kong. What was it like for you when you first arrived?"

Thoughts about her adventures in Wuhan land scrolled through her mind and seemed to stick on that excursion to the Tenglong bat cave during her first week.

"I learned quickly that women are looked down upon as professionals. We are not treated as equals regardless of our knowledge or stature. I had barely settled in at the lab and in my apartment when my mentor, Dr. Wang, invited me on an excursion to the Tenglong Cave. It is about 550 kilometers west of Wuhan. I will never forget the events of that day."

***

Meiling Chen, MD, Ph.D., adjusted her Tyvek biohazard suit but stopped before pulling on her mask. Was there any dignified way she could avoid entering the mammoth hole in the rock looming in front of her?

"Dr. Chen, we must hurry if we are to finish gathering samples before the storm arrives." The expedition leader, Dr. Wang, motioned for her to follow him to the cave's entrance.

As she pulled her mask into place, a short list of cave-associated diseases scrolled across the monitor of Meiling's vivid memory—Tetanus, Rabies, Marburg Hemorrhagic Fever, Tick-borne fevers, Arthropod-borne diseases, possibly Ebola, and she hadn't even considered the many Coronaviruses.

Thoughts of the diseases did not send her into a paralyzing panic attack. But the chief residents of the cave, millions of bats, with their shrill shrieking, pseudo-leather wings, gaping mouths with rows of razor-sharp teeth, including fangs, and their claws—Meiling clamped a gloved hand over her chest to contain the wild percussion solo beating against her sternum.

She took a deep breath, gritted her teeth, and started toward the three men now entering the mouth of the cave.

In her culture, bats symbolized happiness, but the symbol and the referent had no connection in Meiling's mind. How unscientific and absurd was it that a virologist working on a post-doctoral fellowship at the Wuhan Institute of Virology could fear inhabitants of a cave that was the world's largest petri dish for cultivating the viruses she would study?

Absurd, maybe, but not humorous.

After the three men had entered the Tenglong Cave, Dr. Wang turned and studied Meiling as she ambled toward them.

She had tried her best to cover her anxiety with a stoic expression but had the feeling that her mentor's gaze could penetrate her expression like a coronavirus spike penetrates an ACE2 receptor.

Dr. Wang grinned. "Surely our most honored postdoctoral scholar, the first ever from the HKU Medical School, isn't afraid of the viruses in this cave."

"The viruses intrigue me, Doctor, but I have a phobia about bats."

The three men's laughter echoed through the cavern.

Shouldn't they be quieter so as not to awaken the bats? "I do not see the humor."

"Dr. Chen, irony is a form of humor, although the object of the irony may not see it as such." The light mounted above his forehead accentuated the all-knowing smile that stretched across his face.

His look galled her, but it would not be polite to say what she was thinking about his disparaging words and expression.

The Chinese Academy of Sciences had wanted Meiling's expertise in molecular virology—perhaps **coveted** her expertise is a better word choice—to further some of their medical development projects at the Wuhan lab, hence the offer of a fellowship. But so far, all she had seen was the semi-polite but nevertheless condescending attitude toward her displayed by the male researchers, all of whom were from several years to several decades older than Meiling.

She should never have let them know about her bat phobia. It would only put her at a greater disadvantage at the lab. Meiling had been warned by other women in the lab that disadvantages often morphed to sexual harassment from the men in powerful positions.

This was not a good start to her postdoctoral work.

The conversation waned as they fell into a brisk pace. Dr. Wang had emphasized that they must reach the region of interest in less than an hour because the remnants of a dying typhoon might hit Tenglong. The accompanying pressure and humidity changes, coupled with possible thunderstorms, might disturb the bats and bring the excursion to a premature, chaotic end.

The pace slowed as the cave floor narrowed, and large rocks forced them to climb over and detour around obstacles.

Thirty minutes later, Meiling looked up at the cave ceiling for at least the hundredth time. But this time, she shuddered.

Her headlamp revealed dark brown patches covering a third of the ceiling.

Dr. Wang hit one dark patch with the light he carried and then quickly returned the beam to the cave floor. "Only a little farther now until we reach the area of dense population."

Barely audible, a low rumble came from the direction of the mouth of the cave.

At the sound, Dr. Wang picked up the pace. "Another fifty yards and we can start collecting samples."

When Dr. Wang stopped the group, a gentle breeze rippled Meiling's polyethylene sampling bag, now dangling from her left hand.

That was strange. There should not be a breeze a mile into the cave. Was the pressure falling rapidly outside? If so, that might awaken the bats. Were the bats—

A powerful crack slammed against her head like a blow from a hammer.

Bats dropped from the ceiling. Some landed on the floor, surrounding her with their spasming bodies and spreading wings. Others landed on her and clung to her suit with their claws.

Shrieking bats filled the air.

They blocked the light coming from Meiling's headgear sending the cave into near total darkness.

Wings brushed against her suit. Something stung her arm.

A bite from a rabid bat?

Meiling's normal breathing turned to panting. She was hyperventilating but could not stop the process.

Not enough air. She sucked harder at the bit of air in the tiny spaces between millions of bats.

Hyperventilation stole her breath, leaving her only enough for one scream that she could not stifle.

She was suffocating. She had to get out to the thunderstorm, to the rain, to anything but horseshoe bats. Meiling ran pell-mell through an underground river of hideous bats flowing at a wild pace, all headed toward the cave entrance.

She stumbled over rocks but managed to protect her head each time she fell.

It was then that the shrieking bats stole the last thing Meiling still possessed … her sanity.

***

Meiling took a deep breath to slow her rapid pulse. "And that was how I became known as—I will put this in polite terms—the Wuhan Wuss."

"Calling them disparaging names is no way to help your fellow workers. Are you saying there are no encouragers at a research laboratory?" Pastor Lin shook his head. "How do they expect to make progress?"

"I can tell you how they make progress in Chinese research." Meiling blew out a blast of disapproval. "If they can, they steal it—steal it from anyone, even their co-workers at the lab." She paused. "I can illustrate that with a story that also tells you what I did to become CCP enemy number one, a person who must leave China."

Lihua leaned forward and laid her hand on Meiling's bandaged hand. "That is the story we need to hear, as well as the one that tells how you hurt your hand."

Chapter 3

Late evening, January 2, Pastor Lin's home, Hong Kong

Meiling glanced at her bandaged hand. "About how I hurt my hand ... I was trying to hide in the HKU medical research lab when two CCP agents came there looking for me. We have antibacterial ointment in the lab's first aid kit, and I bandaged it well."

Pastor Lin studied Meiling's face for a moment. "Something tells me there was more danger than you are revealing."

Meiling nodded. "They almost found me. But it is more important that I tell you what happened yesterday, nearly two years after the incident at Tenglong Cave. What happened yesterday revealed that my worst fears about accepting the fellowship had been realized, and that convinced me I needed to leave the WIV, which meant I must also leave China."

Pastor Lin glanced at Lihua. "You were right. We do need to hear that story to help her."

Meiling nodded in agreement. "In March, I would have completed my fellowship work, but I could never have turned my most important discovery over to the CCP. They had anticipated a big breakthrough in RNA virus research, including quick, precise techniques for modifying any RNA virus.

"I had become a sought-after speaker for the weekly seminars at the Hubei Engineering and Technology Research Center for Viral Diseases. This was my last seminar before I left Wuhan."

***

The subject Meiling would speak about today was how knowing the commonalities in the molecular structure of RNA viruses permits us to control them—all of them. Her work would allow researchers to kill RNA viruses or change their behavior as desired. This capability applied to all RNA viruses, whether positive strand, negative strand, enveloped, or unenveloped.

The power to control the entire class of viruses now lay in her hands, but that was a discovery she would reveal neither to the power mongers nor the warmongers at the Wuhan lab. And she certainly would not reveal it to the military scavengers, members of the PLA, who attended her presentations, several of whom were in the audience today.

Meiling gave them a forty-five-minute presentation that included enough to whet their appetites but told them neither all that she had discovered nor how to make use of those discoveries. It was time to close.

"That is my theory of molecular viral control. But I must remind you that my work is not yet complete. I must finish verifying that I can put my theory into practice to achieve the desired modifications of any targeted RNA virus."

She was a twenty-eight-year-old, naive virologist when she came to Wuhan. But more than a year and a half later, Meiling was no longer naive. She had noticed that several scientists attending the seminar belonged to a secretive group within the technology research center. These men were members of the military, and rumor had it that they were biowarfare researchers looking for new bioweapons.

Her work, when she finished it, could give them dozens of weapons ranging from Coxsackie Virus, to give humans foot-and-mouth disease, to Ebola or even the Nipah Virus (NiV), one of the deadliest pathogens on the planet.

With Meiling's techniques, gain of function was no longer a slow, protracted process that coaxed nature to make changes. A researcher could design and implement specified changes in days, not years. Any RNA virus would be under their control, and the time to develop and test the pathogenic virus would be shortened by two orders of magnitude.

She had finished her presentation. Now came the dreaded question and answer time, a time when she must tread softly, or she might contradict herself or reveal too much.

One of the military men, a PLA captain, stood. "Dr. Chen, are there any RNA viruses that might be exceptions to your theory, perhaps the more pathogenic cases like the Nipah Virus?"

"No, Captain. The commonalities I exploit belong to the entire class. There are no exceptions."

Her answer seemed to please him, and he sat.

But the uniformed man sitting beside him stood. "Dr. Chen, we know that efforts to apply gain of function to some of the most pathogenic viruses, like Nipah, have been ongoing for a decade or more. Will your techniques replace gain of function?"

The Chinese military was already counting on that very capability by using her research results. It would do no good to deny it. There was no point in lying, thus declaring her work a failure. But this focus on the Nipah Virus was chilling.

"Yes. Instead of gain of function by inducing nature to gradually make changes in a virus, we will specify the desired changes and implement them directly."

Though the man didn't openly smile, his entire face seemed to light up.

The questions ended, and she closed the seminar, but that did not close out the questions and fears conferring in her mind.

Twice now, the military attendees had mentioned the Nipah Virus by name. What were they planning? This was already a deadly virus with a kill rate as high as seventy-five percent. These murderers must never, under any circumstances, be allowed to have her validated theory of RNA virus modifications or the techniques used to implement them.

Meiling, you are just being used as the most expedient means to a deadly and evil end.

The voice inside was right. From here on, there would be no friendly encouragement. Her mentors and others following her research had brought her to a crossroads where she must either finish her work and let the CCP have it or take her research data and documentation and leave. If the latter were her choice, it would put her life in danger.

And, if she ran away, whom could she trust with her research findings? The Americans? Perhaps. But their CDC and FDA had turned corrupt. They would sell her out or enter a lucrative partnership with the highest friendly bidder. Once or twice in the past, that bidder had been the CCP.

Surely there was someone in America she could trust. Maybe someone like Dr. Robert Pierce, the epidemiologist who always stood up to the CDC whenever they were wrong and he was right.

First, Meiling must extract her research data from the lab and get to America safely. Then she would have to hide where the CCP could not find her because once she crossed the line by taking her research and running, the Communists wouldn't just disappear her. They would kill her gruesomely, as they had other would-be defectors. Then they would use her findings to murder as many human beings as necessary for the CCP to establish their global Communist dystopia.

God, please don't let that happen. Don't let me enable

those godless men to carry out their evil plans.

Plans? She needed a plan. Maybe she could send all her research data to her lab back at the HKU Medical School and then delete everything from the Wuhan lab. But the government in China tightly controlled the Internet with help from some American big tech companies. There was no way to ensure they couldn't track her data transfer and simply take her data and Meiling Chen too.

Her research directories on the Wuhan servers contained a little over a terabyte of data. It would fit easily on three 512GB SD cards.

In her locker back at Hong Kong University, Meiling had left several of those cards, each hardly bigger than the tip of her thumb. Once at the school, she could transfer her data from the Wuhan's server to her SD cards. By the time the system administrators discovered the transfer, she could be hiding in Hong Kong.

To disguise the purpose of her leaving, Meiling could use the week of vacation she had been saving. She could pretend to go to Hong Kong to visit her parents. But she must not contact her parents. That might incriminate them.

If she could elude the military police and get on an airplane in Hong Kong, she could fly to the U.S. In America, she would go to a remote location to hide and look for a Christian she could trust, one with connections to scientists like Dr. Robert Pierce.

To protect her research findings, she would only give them to a trusted medical person, one with integrity, one who understood mRNA technology. That person would use her work only for good, and perhaps they could prevent the evil that the CCP and the PLA would use it for. Only one such person came to mind, Dr. Robert Pierce.

***

"Those are the things I've been praying about for the past twenty-four hours, Pastor. I need to escape Hong Kong now and find someone in America who can help me.

"What I did to the entire project at the Wuhan will soon be discovered, and, as I told you, the CCP already has men looking for me. But they don't want just to disappear me. They want to interrogate me, take my data, and kill me.

"Then China gets an entire magazine full of new bio-bullets to load their guns with, enough to kill any segment of the population they can define genetically or if they desire, everyone on the planet who doesn't have the cure that they will most assuredly have."

Chapter 4

Late evening, Pastor Lin's home, Hong Kong

"That is why I am here, trying to escape, Pastor."

"It is a chilling story," Lihua said.

"There is great danger, but we can help you, Meiling." The old preacher pinched his chin, stared at the floor for a few seconds, then looked up at Meiling. "You have three immediate problems to deal with, money, identity, and travel."

She nodded.

"First, let us start with money. What did you do with yours?"

"I withdrew the equivalent of about five hundred American dollars to buy food and incidentals, not unlike what I would do for a trip to Hong Kong. But I do not know how to move the rest of it without that being discovered."

"Let me help. We have a steady stream of people leaving the country, most in similar circumstances to what you face. If you trust us, we have special accounts to hide your money transfers, at least long enough for you to access the money in America and move it to your new American account. But then you must have a safe way to access the money. That could be either through another identity, which you can use for banking and purchases, or a proxy to act on your behalf. Using a proxy can become cumbersome, and the proxy must be trustworthy."

"How do I get another identity?"

"This is illegal, so it is not our first choice, and we do not want you to get in trouble with any American institutions. But if you decide to do this, go to a university and ask students in restaurants, coffee shops, or wherever they congregate how you can get a **temporary ID**. They will realize that you are asking for a state driver's license. Our sources tell us that if you ask a few times, you can almost always find someone to help you.

"But to remain legal, I recommend that you either try the proxy approach or hide in a remote community where it may be difficult for the CCP agents to find you and that you use only your first name initial and your last name for the account. Chen is one of the most common Chinese names. Regardless, the CCP will eventually locate you. But for a person with your credentials, if you contact high-level or well-known medical doctors or officials, they may convince governmental authorities to grant you asylum in America because of the sensitive information and knowledge you have."

"I will take your advice and look for a less populated area. How much money should I take with me?"

"Only take the five hundred dollars with you because you do not want to risk another withdrawal. Also, that amount is small enough that when you disclose it to customs, it will not trigger any alarms."

"What about my flight reservations? I do not know how to do that without them seeing, and I am sure the CCP will be looking."

"Ah, yes. The travel problem. This gets, as the Americans say, a bit dicey."

"Do you mean as in rolling dice and gambling?"

"Yes, it is a gamble with a calculated risk. It has worked many times and only failed once."

So it was not foolproof. How safe was it? "When did it fail, Pastor Lin?"

"The last time we tried this. That was two weeks ago."

Two weeks ago! "That is not encouraging."

"But we have prayer, Meiling. And we only need to get you safely away from the terminal. The CCP will not call the flight back to Hong Kong. They know where it will land, and they have more agents in America than the Russians' SVR has."

"That many? That is not encouraging either."

"Maybe my explanation of how we do this will encourage you. If you fly on Singapore Airlines, they allow you to transfer the ticket to another person if you are unable to go. There is only a small fee and a form to sign. So I will make the reservation in a certain name that appears valid ..."

"But I hope it is not, or you will get this person killed too."

"Do not worry. This person whose name we use is no longer living. We can transfer the ticket to you while you are at the airport. If CCP agents are periodically searching the passenger lists, your name will only appear minutes before you board the plane."

"What if the transfer fails for some reason?"

"We have had several different people book tickets for transferring to another person. It has always worked with the airlines that allow transfers."

"What about the one that failed?"

"That was due to an unexpected event. The flight was delayed for several hours, and that gave the CCP agents too much time to find the passenger after the passenger switch was made. They caught this person as they were boarding."

What the Pastor described should work. A heavy weight seemed to fall from her shoulders. "Thank you so much, Pastor. Getting away by flying to America was beginning to sound so daunting that I had many doubts ... and fears."

"I am glad that I can alleviate your fears, Meiling. I need to call and make the reservations for a flight to San Francisco now before all the seats for tomorrow's flights are taken."

27

Meiling listened closely as he made the call to Singapore Airlines.

"Do you have any seats available for a flight to San Francisco tomorrow?" He paused, and a frown wrinkled his brow. "Nothing at all? ... Would you please check first class also?"

He muted the phone. "She is looking at all flights for first-class seats." He resumed the conversation. "One seat in first class? I will take it."

Pastor Lin completed the reservation for a 1:40 p.m. flight to San Francisco.

"Remember, Meiling, that you will not be visible in the system until you complete the transfer at the airport. That only leaves the CCP agents a short window of time to discover you. As I said, this has never failed to protect any passenger we have helped if that window was short. But we have never helped anyone of your stature, or should I say notoriety."

Meiling sighed. "Like you said. We have prayer."

She spent the night in the guest room of the Lin's house but got up at 6:00 a.m. to make sure everything was in order for her 1:40 p.m. departure from Hong Kong.

After breakfast, Pastor Lin called a taxi for Meiling.

At 10:30 a.m., she said her goodbyes to the Lins, perhaps for the last time.

Meiling had a strategy planned that would minimize her exposure to anyone trying to stop her from leaving.

First, she asked the taxi to drop her off at the loading area near Terminal 1, the terminal from which her flight would leave. Most international flights used Terminal 2. Perhaps that would send anyone looking for her to the wrong terminal.

Once at the terminal, she went to the Singapore Airlines check-in counter to make the change of passenger.

After she made the change to Meiling Chen, she stopped the agent from creating the boarding pass and from checking baggage.

"Miss Chen, are you sure you don't want to check your luggage?"

"I've got some things in my suitcase that I just remembered I need to get out and put in my carry-on. I'll come back in a while and finish checking in."

"Where is your bag?"

Now the lady at the counter was getting too nosey. Meiling had no suitcase.

She nodded toward a group of suitcases a few feet away.

The agent looked puzzled but didn't reply.

While the agent at the counter was busy helping another passenger, Meiling hurried toward the self-check-in kiosks. Now she could wait until nearer to departure time to get her boarding pass. Hopefully, that would make it less likely that her pursuers could find her before take-off.

She waited to check in at a kiosk until thirty minutes before boarding started for her flight. With her boarding pass and passport in hand, she cleared security and arrived at the gate in time to hear the early boarding announcement for first-class passengers.

As she approached the agent near the jetway, who was taking passenger information for the flight manifest, Meiling turned to take a last look at the Hong Kong terminal.

A gruff voice drew her attention. It came from a man having an intense discussion with one of the gate agents.

She had heard that voice before.

Meiling showed her boarding pass and ID, then scurried down the jetway and prayed that if the man were a CCP agent, he wouldn't try to board the plane to get her.

Nothing unusual happened during boarding. But after all, passengers were onboard, the captain came on the audio system.

"There will be a short delay because one of our passengers needs to disembark before we take off. Give us a few minutes, and we'll be on our way."

Was Meiling the disembarking passenger? Was someone coming to take her off the plane?

She tried to pretend the announcement did not concern her, but that was impossible. Thinking that any moment a gruff-voiced CCP goon would come charging down the aisle to arrest her was driving her insane.

Meiling looked up at a flight attendant standing nearby. "Excuse me, while we're still at the gate, may I use the lavatory?"

"Yes, but don't dilly dally because we can't proceed with departure procedures until you are back in your seat."

Meiling hurried to the lavatory and, once inside, locked the door and checked the time on her cell. How long should she delay? She decided on four minutes.

Hiding in the lavatory probably would not save her if the CCP came looking for her on this flight. But if they did not see her, maybe they would go back to the terminal to look.

She tried to appear calm when she returned to her seat, but her heart was still beating on her sternum like a prisoner trying to break free from some prison.

Someone holding their carry-on bag sauntered down the aisle and left through the open door to the jetway.

The door closed, the whirring sounds of the jet bridge came from outside, seatbelt lights came on, and the big 777 backed away from the terminal.

But Meiling's pulse did not slow until the plane lifted off the runway.

So they had not found her in time to stop her.

Thank you, God, and thank you, Pastor Lin.

When exhaustion hit a few minutes later, Meiling reclined her seat and dozed off.

She woke and checked the time. She had slept for six hours.

The twelve-hour flight meant she would arrive at San Francisco around 9:45 a.m. the previous date. She would have to live that terror-filled date again. Fortunately, she would not live it in Hong Kong.

But the gruff-voiced man at the gate meant the CCP knew she was on this airplane.

Does that mean a CCP agent will be waiting for me at the gate in San Francisco?

Chapter 5

January 2, KPPR TV News Studio, Bend, Oregon

R yan Adams stood behind the podium where he had just delivered his weather forecast for the Bend area. A large map of Central Oregon lit the screen behind him. Now it was time for his closing summary.

"Folks, the Arctic Express is on its way. The cold air begins to arrive in about thirty-six hours. The leading edge will likely bring record-breaking snow, followed by several days of frigid weather. We could see ten below here in Bend and fifteen below in the outlying areas, so bundle up, stock up, and take care of yourself and your neighbors."

Amanda Barrett, the news anchor, closed the broadcast.

The cameras and lights dimmed, and the usual chatter between the news team members began.

"Ryan, how's your website, Dionysius Street, going?" Amanda slid a sheaf of papers into her desk. "Have you scheduled a debate with that atheist from Yale yet?"

"Amanda, debates turn into arguments. People want to know who won and who lost. They tend to forget the most important things about the discussion. I've found something more interesting and, hopefully, more beneficial to focus on."

Amanda's wide blue eyes looked rather surprised. "More beneficial? What's that?"

"A lot of folks have wild ideas and fears about how this world or this age ends. The climate-change scare generated part of that fear. The COVID pandemic a few years ago added to it. We survived both **catastrophes**, despite ourselves. But that leaves me wondering what's next."

"This does sound interesting."

"There are three factions all seeking world domination, the wealthy elitists, the political globalists, and the Chinese Communist Party, the CCP. They all cooperate to a degree when it's in their mutual interests. But COVID has degenerated to the common cold, and the political pendulum has swung to the right for now. So what's coming next?"

"Ryan, what do you think might come next?"

"I'm a weather forecaster, not a prophet."

"But you're also becoming a well-known apologist. Surely you have thoughts about what's in store for us next on planet Earth."

"I'm most concerned about the CCP. No matter how you slice it, the evidence says they were responsible for the COVID pandemic. But it turned out that COVID-19 could be quashed by any thinking doctor or medical researcher.

"But the CCP still believes that Communism must be the form for a global government. And the CCP is more evil and dangerous than the wealthy elitists, the climate alarmists, or anyone else seeking to dominate this planet.

"I believe the CCP will unleash a biowarfare weapon that will make COVID look like child's play. They will up their game, using some virus with a death rate of, say, fifty percent instead of the tiny fraction of one percent with COVID. And if they can strike fear into every heart on the planet, and then offer a therapeutic for the virus, they might even cause the wealthy globalists to surrender to the CCP."

"A fifty percent kill rate? What kind of disease are you talking about?" Amanda said.

"I'm no expert, but I've heard that the hemorrhagic fevers, like Ebola and Marburg, have a case fatality rate of thirty to fifty percent. Something more common in the U.S., Hantavirus, is thirty to forty percent fatal. Shall I continue?"

"For heaven's sake, no. Just thinking about something that deadly makes me shiver."

"Well, it makes me want to write a blog post about the likelihood that China will cook up something new at their Wuhan lab and turn it loose on the world." He paused. "I'd give my right arm for a reliable source of info in China. But their surveillance system is better than Orwell's Big Brother in his novel 1984. It'll probably keep loose lips from sinking their apocalypse."

Amanda didn't reply.

"I have tomorrow off. Maybe I'll write that post and see what kind of responses I get."

Chapter 6

Two days later

Ryan winced and covered his ears as that song about Christmas, snow coming down, and a man pleading for his love to come home, played at full volume on his alarm clock. He slapped the snooze button then sat up on the side of the bed to turn the alarm off before the song could play again.

Christmas was over, and so was New Year's Day. It was January 4, 8:00 a.m., according to his alarm, and he needed to load a new flash drive with some other genre of music into his MP3 player on the alarm. Considering the weather that was coming, songs like *Let It Snow* seemed appropriate.

After working on his blog post until 2:00 a.m., eight o'clock was too early to be starting his day.

When he reached for the alarm to remove the flash drive, his cell, lying on the nightstand, buzzed and played his incoming call alarm.

The caller ID indicated Amanda was calling.

What did she want? Probably a weather update.

Amanda didn't trust the new forecaster they'd hired right out of college. The young woman was bright. She just needed some more experience.

Ryan picked up the call. "Hello, Amanda. To what do I owe this honor at such an ungodly hour?"

"You must have been working on that blog post about China's newest model of the coronavirus."

"Something like that. But why are you calling?"

"Evidently, you haven't heard any news this morning."

"No. What's up? Did Kirsten bust her forecast?"

"No. You need to go to your laptop, click on your bookmark for The Epoch Times, and read the headlines."

"The Epoch Times?"

"Just do it, Ryan."

Headlines: Scientist Employed at the Wuhan Institute of Virology Allegedly Defects with Deadly Virus in Tow

"You've got to be kidding me."

"Watch out what you wish for, Ryan."

"What do you mean?"

"If I remember correctly, you said you wished you had a good source of info in China. The article is fairly short. Read it and tell me what you think."

He scanned down the article. Meiling Chen, MD, Ph.D., molecular virology expert ... ripped off her research and a nasty virus ... defected to U.S. ... landed in San Francisco and disappeared.

Ryan chuckled. "She doesn't have any deadly virus, Amanda. The CCP is just using that to try to get the U.S. to arrest her and maybe return her to them."

"She sure looks young. Maybe too young for you."

"I said I was looking for a source of information, not for you to try, once again, to match me with—"

"Take another look at that picture, Ryan. Look at those eyes, intelligent, intense. She's just your type."

"It says she's twenty-nine. I wonder how a woman, especially one that young, got into the inner sanctum of the CCP's biowarfare brain trust."

"If you find her, maybe you can ask her. I just wanted to let you know about this interesting coincidence. Changing the subject, did you get your blog article posted?"

"I did. 2:00 a.m. last night."

"So that's why you're so grouchy this morning. What did you post?"

"Go read it for yourself. I can use another hit on my blog. It's been languishing over the holidays. I guess dry subjects like apologetics and end-time events can't compete with Jesus' birth."

Amanda laughed. "It's not really funny, but somehow, I don't think most Americans were thinking about Jesus' birth over the holidays. Well, I've got to go now. It's almost time for the morning report."

"Thanks for the heads up. But with every CCP agent on the West Coast, along with the FBI, all after Dr. Chen, it won't be me she talks to. But I wish the young woman luck. She probably had good reasons for leaving China, and, as for the luck, she's going to need it."

After Amanda ended the call, Ryan pulled back the curtains by his desk.

The snow had started out as large, puffy flakes gently falling to the white ground. Now, the snowflakes were smaller but increasing in intensity. By tonight the wind would pick up, bringing blizzard conditions to Central Oregon.

This was a good day to stay inside and work on his blog.

He dressed and groomed while another pot of coffee brewed. Ryan took a mug filled with the rich blend and returned to his desk to write.

Ryan was hungry. His coffee was cold, and his wall clock said 8:30 p.m. Where had the day gone? He had written ten thousand words which he would use for several blog posts, but he hadn't even stopped for lunch or dinner.

When his stomach growled a loud complaint, he stood to get something to eat.

Before he reached the kitchen, the doorbell rang.

Chapter 7

Ryan turned toward his front door.

At nearly 9:00 p.m., it was dark, cold, and snowing. Who would be ringing his doorbell? Was it somebody needing help because they were stuck in the snow?

He scampered to the door and peered out the peephole.

A small figure stuffed into a long, hooded puffy coat stood alone on his doorstep.

He opened the door and snow swirled into his living room. "May I help you?"

"If you are Mr. Ryan Adams, you may be the only person who **can** help me."

Her voice held hints of both British and Asian accents. She had large, almond-shaped eyes. Tresses of black hair that had escaped from the hood waved in the breeze.

"It's cold out there. Please come in and tell me how Ryan Adams can help you."

The young woman stepped in and closed the door.

She pulled the hood down.

Recognition! The jolt hit Ryan like the shock he'd once received from a 110-volt electrical outlet.

Standing in front of him was the Chinese defector, Dr. Chen. Amanda's description was spot on, but what was she doing on his doorstep?

"May I take your coat?"

"First, Mr. Adams, let me warn you that helping me might bring danger to yourself. I can leave now if you are having any reservations."

Her intense brown eyes seemed to peer deeply into him, but they were not harsh or judgmental. More like all-knowing.

Ryan scanned her face more slowly this time. He wouldn't call Dr. Meiling Chen drop-dead gorgeous, but no matter how he looked at her, there wasn't one thing he would change. She was perfect.

And, dude, you are being perfectly adolescent.

The annoying voice inside was right, but at this moment, he felt like an adolescent.

"Mr. Adams, you do not have to stare like that and wonder about me. Just ask me your questions."

"Uh, yeah. But just call me Ryan."

Her lips displayed a brief smile. It further enhanced her incredible beauty. How would a woman like Dr. Chen fare in a land where men ruled the roost while they outnumbered women by thirty or forty million?

He had to stop staring at her.

"Well, Ryan …"

"Dr. Chen—"

"Please, call me Meiling."

He nodded. "Meiling, what do you need, and why do you think I'm the person who can help you?"

"I was searching for Christian websites run by people in this area. I made a list of them. After I saw you present the weather on TV and heard some comments you made, I put you at the top of my list. When I went to your website, I found that you are a Christian and an apologist."

"Christian, yes. Apologist—not by formal training. I'm self-taught. Meiling, do you follow Jesus too?"

"Yes, but I am a new follower and one that has made many mistakes. But can we talk about that another time?"

"Is that why you wanted my help?"

"Not exactly. On your website, you posted two interviews with Dr. Robert Pierce, the researcher who helped develop mRNA vaccine technology."

"I did interview Dr. Pierce, but—"

"So you know him?"

"I do."

"Do you know him well enough to contact him and inquire about a possible meeting?"

"Yes. And if *you* are attending the meeting, he will almost certainly agree to it."

"Then you *are* the answer to my prayer."

Interesting, but it was unlikely that Ryan Adams was the answer to any woman's prayer. He'd never had a deep enough relationship with a member of the opposite sex for that to be true.

"Maybe you should tell me more of your story, so I understand how I can help you."

"Then I should start at the beginning while I was doing molecular virology research at HKUMed, Hong Kong University Medical School."

"Before you start, would you like something warm to drink, coffee, tea, hot chocolate?"

"Do you mean American tea? I mean as in *not* milk tea?"

"What I have is *not* served with milk. It's a popular blend of black tea with orange and cinnamon. It comes from Seattle."

"That sounds wonderful."

"Great. Let's move to the kitchen, and you can start your story while I start the tea."

While Ryan made the tea, Meiling launched into a somewhat improbable story that ended up with a brilliant researcher from HKUMed being given a postdoctoral fellowship in the heart of Communist China, the Wuhan Institute of Virology.

"You were from Hong Kong. Did the senior researchers at the institute trust you?"

"When the CCP and their military, the PLA, are involved, there is no trust, only manipulation of people for control."

Ryan handed her a cup of tea. She sipped and smiled. "I'm going to abandon milk tea."

"After recent events, I believe you already have."

Meiling's smile faded.

Dude, she left her home for good. You didn't need to remind her.

He shook off the reminder and tried to focus on Meiling. "Why would the CCP or PLA bring a researcher from rebellious Hong Kong to Wuhan?"

"Though it's not a military facility, the PLA is involved at the Wuhan lab. Several years ago, the U.S. published a report saying that the PLA operated thirty facilities involved in research and development, production, and testing of biological warfare weapons. But that list did not include the Wuhan Institute of Virology. Since then, they have learned that the WIV collaborated on secret projects with China's PLA and engaged in classified research. But the PLA's primary domain is the Academy of Military Science in Beijing, where they modify human beings, made in God's image, changing them into monsters that can dominate on the battlefield."

Her gaze turned from merely intense to something frightening. "If what I've heard is true, the PLA's experiments make Hitler and Mengele look like angels."

Thinking about what Meiling described tied an overhand knot in his gut. "Knowing all that, why did you accept the fellowship to go to Wuhan, Meiling?"

"Senior researchers at Wuhan heard of my work in molecular virology. Apparently, they believed I was on the verge of a breakthrough that would simplify manipulation of RNA viruses, or for them, gain of function."

"Are you on the verge?"

"After nearly two years at Wuhan, I am well past the breakthrough, but that's something I've used every ability I have to conceal. That's not easy to do in an environment where you are being surveilled, where people want to steal your findings, and no one trusts anyone."

"If I may ask, what were your findings, and what did the PLA want to do with them?"

Meiling reached a hand across the table and laid it over his. "Ryan, I am willing to answer your question, but only if you willingly accept the danger the answers bring. If they find out that you know about my discoveries, the CCP and the PLA will target you, and you will never be safe again."

Ryan gave her his warmest smile. "The point of no return—I believe I already crossed that when a certain young woman pulled down her hood, and I realized who was standing in front of me."

Meiling shook her head and sighed. "I hoped my picture would not be circulated so quickly. That means the agents they sent looking for me will find me sooner than I expected. They have too many sources of information in America to allow me to hide very long."

"What about the answers to my questions?"

She removed her hand from his. "My breakthrough allowed us, using my molecular-level approaches, to modify much more easily any RNA virus. I know some of the applications the CCP plans for my work—things like large-scale genocide."

"Genocide? So they plan to release a virus into areas where the target race lives?"

"No. My techniques can use the genome to target victims by biological race. If you have the genome, you get sick." She paused. "If you have read any of the CCP's planning documents, you will see that this fits their plan for communist world domination through unrestricted warfare."

"So they just wipe out a race? What about the progeny of mixed-race marriages?"

"Some of their children will undoubtedly be killed too. With the CCP, collateral damage is not a concern." She blew out a sharp sigh. "Ryan, we are literally dealing with Satan here. The evil is so oppressive that I could feel it as I walked the halls of the Wuhan Institute. It almost drove me to leave before I finished my work."

"I believe you. I've read about Americans who visited the old USSR during the Cold War. They had similar experiences. That's what happens when you remove God from a society." He paused. "So what's next?"

"I am carrying all my research with me. One and a half terabytes on three 512 GB micro-SD memory cards. We need to place a copy of the data in the hands of someone we trust, someone who will understand my research findings when I explain them, and someone who will only use the research for good."

Her use of the pronoun *we* spoke volumes. "Someone we trust? You mean Dr. Pierce?"

"Yes, if he is willing to accept the danger from the Chinese."

"A little danger has never deterred Robert Pierce. He takes on the dagger-wielding American media on a weekly basis. They have tried and failed to take his medical license. But I believe we can keep our meeting with him off anyone's radar screen. I have an ex-military pilot friend who flies his Gulfstream out of Redmond. With his help, we can meet secretly."

"Ryan, do you know if Dr. Pierce has access to a medical research lab?"

"He is part owner of a lab near his house in Colorado and does his research there."

"Is it biosafety level three or level four?"

"Officially, it's listed as BSL-3, but he upgraded the lab. I know Dr. Pierce has worked on level four pathogens and seemed comfortable doing that ... if anyone can ever be comfortable working with those little demons."

"Can we arrange to meet with Dr. Pierce and turn my work over to him as soon as possible?"

"I'm going to call Dr. Pierce now using my sat phone. It's less likely your CCP friends can—"

"Please, do not call them my friends."

The fierce look on Meiling's face said she would fight evil and not run when the battle grew intense. Meiling was someone Ryan could count on in a battle.

"Sorry. I just wanted to say that the sat phone call is harder to hack, especially if hackers are unaware that Dr. Pierce and I both have sat phones."

Ryan pulled his phone from a pocket in his coat which hung on the back of his chair.

"Sit here beside me, Meiling. I'll turn on the speakerphone so you can join the conversation. That should speed things up a bit."

She pulled another chair beside him and sat.

Ryan set his phone in front of them and dialed Dr. Pierce's number.

"It's about 9:30 p.m. Mountain Time. Pierce is an early-to-bed, early-to-rise guy. If he's in bed, I may have to leave a message."

On the fourth ring, someone picked up the call.

"This is Robert Pierce. Is that you calling, Ryan?"

"Yes, sir. This call is a bit sensitive. I have someone with me whom I'm sure you will want to talk to. I'll let her explain the sensitivity issues. Dr. Pierce, here is the young woman I met this evening, Dr. Meiling Chen."

"The Chinese defector? The one from Wuhan?"

"Dr. Pierce, I did not defect, I'm not from Wuhan, and I do not have a deadly virus with me."

Pierce was silent for a few moments. "But that's the story the media is telling."

"Most of the media is either controlled or highly influenced by the CCP. I am a medical researcher from Hong Kong University, but I was offered a postdoctoral fellowship at the Wuhan Institute of Virology to perform molecular virology research, research applicable to RNA viruses."

"That clarifies several things, Dr. Chen, but didn't you realize your research would likely end up in some new biowarfare weapon?"

"I am not naïve, Dr. Pierce, but they believed that I was because of my age and the fact that I was working at HKUMed. I am certain that I completed my work at Wuhan without anyone at the institute knowing that or accessing certain findings that I kept hidden. Recently, my seminars have all ended with probing questions that deeply concerned me. The questions came mostly from military members who attended. I felt threatened and quickly flew back to Hong Kong University, logged in to the Wuhan lab, and retrieved my research data. Then I destroyed all data for the entire RNA research project residing on the Wuhan servers."

"That couldn't have made the CCP happy. And that must have been when you jumped ship."

"Yes. I jumped ship immediately. Within hours, they sent some men to HKU to kill me, and they almost did. But with help from a secret organization in Hong Kong, I made it to the U.S., where I discovered Ryan Adams and his interviews with you."

"How exactly can I help you, Dr. Chen?"

"Please, call me Meiling." She paused. "I need a trustworthy scientist in the U.S. who can understand my work, someone who will protect it and use it only for good purposes. But I must warn you, Dr. Pierce, collaborating with me and hosting my research data will eventually cause the CCP, or the PLA, to target you. It may place your life in danger."

"Since the COVID-19 pandemic a few years ago, any research that bucks the CCP's narrative seems to put one's career or life in danger." He paused. "Meiling, I would be honored to host your research and offer my lab to help you advance your work ... under your direction, of course."

"Ryan has told me a bit about your lab. But how strong is your lab security?"

"A special forces team, like Navy SEALS, could probably breach security and enter the lab, but any lesser force would not make it in, and they would wish they hadn't if they did."

"I agree, Ryan said. "We won't find better security at any privately owned lab in North America."

"Then we should do this quickly," Meiling said. "As soon as possible."

"If I can schedule a flight with my pilot for tomorrow night, can you pick us up at Rocky Mountain Metro? To avoid attention, we will probably schedule arrival around midnight Mountain Time."

"Give me an arrival time when you have it, and I'll be there to pick you up."

"Meiling and I will need to stay at the lab for a few days."

"That's not a problem," Dr. Pierce said. "We have temporary living quarters on-site within our security perimeter."

Meiling laid her hand on his shoulder. "Ryan, I am interfering with your job and your career. Can you take off from work with such short notice?"

"Thanks for your concern, but it's not a problem. We're training an intern meteorologist at the station. She'll be more than happy to fill in for me."

"Well, we're all set then," Pierce said. "Let us know when you have an ETA."

"Will do, and thanks so much, Dr. Pierce."

She removed her hand from Ryan's shoulder. "Yes, thank you, Dr. Pierce. You may have saved my life. I will pray that I do not endanger yours."

Ryan ended the call and studied Meiling's face for a moment. "Any questions before I call my pilot, Radley Baker?"

"No questions. I am just amazed at how many resources you have to draw on and the freedom you have to do that in America."

"I fear that we Americans take our liberty for granted. We need to remember that at any given time, a free America is only one generation from dying." Ryan keyed Baker's number into his sat phone. "I'm turning on the speakerphone, Meiling."

"Baker here."

"Baker, this is Ryan. Is there any possibility of chartering your Gulfstream for a flight tomorrow night?"

"If it's important, I can free up a few hours tomorrow night. What's up?"

"Baker, if you were still in the military, what I'm about to tell you would be top-secret compartmentalized info. We must not compromise it no matter the cost."

"Ryan, if you're trying to get my attention, you've got it. But don't tell me more than I need to know."

"I have with me Dr. Meiling Chen and her research data."

"Is that the Chinese defector that the CCP says stole classified info and fled to the U.S. with a deadly virus?"

"It is all lies," Meiling said.

Ryan leaned toward the phone. "The information belongs to Meiling—uh ... Dr. Chen, and she cannot let it get into the hands of the CCP, PLA, or any of their agents. That could put the rest of the world at risk."

"The plot thickens and the stakes rise. Where am I taking Dr. Chen?"

"We need you to deliver Meiling and me to Dr. Robert Pierce's lab outside of Denver."

"This will be the third time I've flown that route. Still using Rocky Mountain Metro?"

"Yes. And, Baker, how does your schedule look for the next couple of days?"

"This is a slow time of year for me. I have all day tomorrow, tomorrow night, and the next day."

"Great. We never know when threats might emerge to change our plans."

"Adams, I need to know if there are imminent threats here." His voice crescendoed on imminent threats.

"Settle down, Baker. The people chasing Dr. Chen will probably strike the minute they locate her. She tried to hide when she entered the U.S., and we don't know when they might find her. But it shouldn't be until after we deliver her to Dr. Pierce."

"I suggest you make the delivery ASAP," Baker said.

"And that's what I'm suggesting, a midnight special delivery tomorrow. What time do we need to be at Roberts Field in Redmond?"

"Not later than 9:00 p.m. It's an hour and a half flight to Rocky Mountain Metro." Baker paused. "But, Ryan, if you encounter any trouble between now and then, call me. I may be able to help."

"Will do, Baker. We'll see you tomorrow at nine o'clock. I'll call if anything changes."

Ryan ended the call.

Meiling laid her hand on his arm. "Once again, I am amazed by all the resources you have at your disposal."

"We have an incredible group of patriots here in Central Oregon, people who love America. And they **are** pretty amazing."

And so was Meiling. She was beyond bright, a world-class scientist, but she wasn't cold and aloof. She was warm and open. She obviously liked eye contact when talking to people, and touching was not taboo.

Dude, you can't let anything happen to her. She's one in seven billion.

The voice inside was right. Meiling Chen was one of a kind on planet Earth. But in duping the CCP at Wuhan, Meiling had probably made the CCP's top ten most wanted list, a notoriety few survived. And Ryan would do whatever it took to keep her among the living few.

The next few days or hours would tell him how much that might cost.

Chapter 8

Ryan thought he and Meiling had taken care of the most important matters with his two phone calls, but the young woman sitting by him had escaped China with almost nothing but herself and her research data. She probably had other needs.

"Is there anything you weren't able to get or bring with you? It sounds like you left Hong Kong in a hurry."

Meiling nodded. "I bought a warm coat today before I came to your place, but the stores were closing, so there are a few things I still need."

"There's a twenty-four-hour Super Walmart at the south end of Bend. It's only three miles from here. It won't have the most fashionable clothes, but it will have just about anything you might need."

Ryan stood and ambled to the living room window.

Meiling followed him.

He drew the curtains back a few inches.

The streetlights produced a corona in the heavy, wind-driven snow.

"We should go to the store now, Meiling. We already have near-blizzard conditions, and it's only going to get worse. My Highlander can handle six to eight inches of snow, but if the drifts grow higher—I don't want to get us stuck in a snow drift."

She stood behind him and peered over his shoulder. "Are you sure it is okay to drive in this?"

"If we go now, we'll be fine. While you put on your coat, I'm going to get my Sig Sauer, just in case."

"Sig Sauer? Does it help with snow?"

He chuckled. "No. It's a nine-millimeter handgun, a gun Navy SEALS have used for years."

"A gun? Is that necessary?"

"I don't know. But if someone trapped us, would you prefer to put up a fight or surrender?"

"I—I get your point." She picked up her coat.

Ryan strode to his bedroom, took his gun from the safe, and slipped it into the holster that rode against the small of his back.

He pulled his biggest and heaviest coat from the closet and put it on.

When he returned to the living room, Meiling scanned his entire body while a frown remained between her large, almond-shaped eyes. "I do not see your gun."

"You're not supposed to. I have what's called a concealed carry permit. No one will see my gun unless I need to use it."

"Come on, Meiling." He led her out to the garage.

Two minutes later, the Highlander was slipping and sliding in the deep snow, but its intelligent all-wheel drive kept the SUV mostly under control.

Five minutes later, Ryan parked near the door of the Super Walmart in a mostly deserted parking lot, and they got out.

"Let's hurry. This could be a record-breaking snowstorm, and the manager may want to close early and send the workers home."

At his words, Meiling strode briskly through the snow toward the automatic doors. Halfway to the door, her foot slipped in the deep snow. She was going down.

Ryan hooked her arm to catch her, and he pulled her back to her feet. "Let's see if we can find some hiking boots for you. Something suitable for snow."

. L. WEGLEY

She flashed him a smile. "That does not sound very fashionable."

"Like I told you, this isn't the best store for fashion. But you can find clothes to meet all your basic needs, even hiking boots."

Inside the store, Ryan picked up a handbasket.

Meiling stopped and scanned the interior layout, and she turned to her right to walk toward the ladies' clothing section. She picked up a sweater, examined it, put it in the basket Ryan carried, and then stopped.

She looked up at Ryan, and her cheeks turned a rosy red. "You will probably learn a lot more about me in the coming days. But, Ryan, you are not going to learn it here." She nodded her head to her left.

Ryan's gaze followed the direction of Meiling's nod. They were standing on the edge of the ladies' underwear department.

"I'll be in electronics when you're done here." He handed her the shopping basket and noted the relief in Meiling's eyes before he turned toward the big, flat-screen TV mounted high on the wall.

A few minutes later, Meiling found him. "Show me what kind of boots I need for snow and cold."

After Ryan helped her find a suitable pair of hiking boots, the shopping basket was nearly overflowing. But the underwear was carefully buried and out of sight.

So how was this going to work at checkout? When she pulled out the underwear, her top-secret info would be compromised. Maybe he should approach this subject by coming in the side door.

"How are you going to pay for this?"

"Did I not tell you about the proxy accounts and moving my money through them to an American bank?"

"I don't think so."

"All my money came with me, so I will pay for my purchases."

Dude, you don't have to pay or help her check out, so get lost.

"And I will wait for you by the exit." He paused. "Meiling, after you checkout, you should go to into the women's restroom and change into those hiking boots. The walk out to the car will be much less slippery if you do."

She nodded and headed toward the nearest checker.

In three or four minutes, Meiling emerged from the women's restroom. Her slacks covered most of the hiking boots, which added an inch to her height.

Ryan couldn't help but notice the impact the extra height had on her elegant beauty. When God chose to give one of his creations something near perfection—her personality, mannerisms, and physical beauty—the impact was incredible.

It was even more incredible that Ryan, the person charged with her safety, could be so distracted from his duty.

Meiling smiled as she approached, carrying two shopping bags and her purse slung over her shoulder. "I am ready for the snow, Ryan."

"Then let's go before we get snowed in here." He stepped within range of the door's motion sensor and bowed, motioning her through the opening door.

She giggled at his melodramatic, genteel behavior. The giggling stopped when she stepped to the door.

The parking lot lights shone dimly in the near whiteout conditions.

She whirled, grabbed Ryan's arm with her free hand, and pulled him back into the store.

"Meiling, what's—"

"There was a man standing by your SUV and another car behind it with its lights shining on your car."

"Are you sure it was my SUV they were examining?"

"Yes."

"Then let's move over by the entrance door to that dark area where they can't see us. We'll watch them. It might only be some high school kids up to mischief."

She pulled him by the arm to the shadowy area. "I do not think so."

Ryan stopped and studied the area by his Highlander. "Look, the guy outside just walked back to the passenger side of the other car. Looks like a big four-wheel-drive vehicle."

Meiling curled her free arm around his waist and clung tightly to him.

Ryan lifted her chin until their gazes locked. "I need you to tell me what you're thinking."

Even in the shadows, agony lined her usually smooth face. "It is them. The CCP agents."

"But that's not possible. They couldn't have found us, linked you to me, and been checking out my vehicle in a Walmart parking lot in only a few hours."

"But you do not know them like I do, Ryan."

"And they don't even know I exist yet."

"They are masters at surveillance. In China, they know everything about everybody."

"There's a lot they still haven't found out about you, Meiling."

"You are not listening to me, Ryan."

"Okay. I'm listening. How could they have found you and linked you to me in such a short time?"

She slid her arm from his waist and took his hand. "I do not think you understand whom we are dealing with. The CCP plants Chinese people in positions where they can bribe Americans who hold advantageous positions in government, business, even the airlines. One compromised airline employee could query the system and find that I took a flight from Oakland to Redmond. With a bit more effort, they could bribe or persuade someone to find that I rented a car in Redmond. Most rental cars can be tracked. When I drove to your house, I led them to both of us. I should have been more careful."

"It's not your fault, Meiling. But now we need to try to get your things at my house and find a place to hide until Baker flies us to Denver tomorrow night."

"But they could be waiting out there somewhere to kill us."

"Or to capture you. Either way, we can't let them succeed. You've got to get your research to Pierce's lab. Let's get your things at my house if we can. Then we'll disappear for a few hours."

"I am so sorry that I have endangered you. I should have known they would find me quickly."

"And if you had known, what could you have done differently to ensure your safety?"

She didn't reply.

"Meiling, regardless of how this plays out, I'm glad you came to me for help, and I pray that God will enable me to deliver you safely to Dr. Pierce. Come on. Let's go."

He took Meiling's hand and stepped toward the door.

It slid open.

There were no signs of the suspected CCP agents, so Ryan hurried hand-in-hand with Meiling through the blowing snow to his SUV.

He hit the fob to unlock the doors, and they both slid in.

Ryan took Meiling's two shopping bags and dropped them in the back floorboard. "Buckle in tightly. The snow's deeper, and it's drifting. We're going to slide around a lot."

He hit the ignition and the lights and headed for the parking lot exit that was the shortest route to his house.

When they left the glare of the parking lot lights, visibility improved a little, and Meiling gasped.

"What is it?"

"The car coming toward us—the headlights look like ..."

The car turned off the street and disappeared.

"You're right. It **was** them." He yanked the wheel to the right, and the rear end of his Highlander swung side to side as the wheels spun in deep snow.

A few seconds later, the now familiar headlights of the big four-wheel-drive turned onto the street ahead of them and rushed straight at them.

"Hang on, Meiling." Ryan cut to his right down an alleyway to the next street. They pulled out onto the street and tried to turn left toward his house. Once again, the four-wheel-drive appeared ahead of them.

"They keep cutting us off. I think they're trying to prevent me from reaching my house."

Meiling turned toward him. "Ryan, they may have put a tracker on your car at the parking lot."

"You're right."

"What do you plan to do?" The anxiety in Meiling's voice cut into his heart like a knife.

He had to keep her safe, but only one desperate way to do that came to mind.

"Their four-wheel-drive can outmaneuver me in the snow. Eventually, they will cut us off and run us down."

"No. We cannot let it end like that."

"You're right. And if my plan works, it won't end badly." Ryan ran over the curb and off the street. He cut between two trees and ended up on another street which snaked its way to the southeast.

"What are you doing?"

"Buying us a few minutes before they can find us again. Does your coat keep you warm when we're outside in these temperatures?"

"Yes. So far, it has."

"Will it keep you warm enough to walk a mile? That's about twenty minutes in this wind and snow."

"I think so."

"Then unbuckle when I tell you to. We'll both jump out and run down the road."

"But they will just follow our tracks."

"In these conditions, with the wind still picking up, the drifting snow should hide our tracks. This is where I played as a kid, Meiling. We're at the edge of a network of lava tubes. The temperature will drop to minus ten tonight, but back in the cave, it will be in the low forties."

"Ryan, I have one question for you."

"What's that?"

"Are there bats in this cave?"

He got the distinct impression his answer should be no. But this was the Skeleton Cave, and the state limited access to it because of the large bat population.

Ryan glanced at Meiling.

Even in the shadowy interior of the car, he could see the terror displayed in her wide eyes and etched in the lines on her face.

If she balked at the cave, they were in serious trouble. He blew out a sharp breath but didn't answer her question about bats.

Meiling studied his face then shook her head. "Ryan, I cannot do this."

Chapter 9

If Ryan couldn't change Meiling's mind about the cave, they would be found when the tracker led the CCP goons to them. That would happen in the next few minutes.

To change her mind, he needed to understand her phobia. "Meiling, are you afraid of bats biting you, of the diseases they carry, or just afraid of bats in general?"

"All of the above."

"I guarantee you the CCP is a greater threat to you than the bats in Skeleton Cave. And if you could see into their Marxist souls, those atheistic murderers would look uglier than any bat in the cave. Regardless, we can't wait any longer. Let's go."

Meiling got out of the car, closed the door, and met him in front of his SUV. Her rapid breathing sounded above the whining of the wind.

Blowing and drifting snow would soon cover their tracks, and visibility had deteriorated to a few feet. This would work if Meiling would come with him.

Ryan took her hand and tugged.

She resisted. "I think I am hyperventilating."

Desperate situations sometimes called for desperate measures. "We can't stay here any longer. There are two ways we can do this, Meiling. I can hit you over the head with my gun, and you'll never have to see the bats."

"Ryan, you wouldn't. I trusted you to—"

"All right, we'll do it this way." He scooped her up in his arms and jogged slowly through the snow toward the cave.

She circled his neck with her arms and held on tightly.

Warm tears dripped onto his neck.

"Ryan?"

He didn't reply.

"Ryan, please talk to me. You need to put me down, or you are going to fall and get hurt."

He slowed to a stop and let Meiling slide from his arms onto her feet.

"Please forgive me for being such a coward and for being so selfish that I endangered your life."

"You're anything but a coward. You're simply a woman with a phobia about bats. If you'll promise to come along voluntarily, I'll take you to a place in the cave that's much warmer, and that lies beyond the bats. If you don't look up after we enter, you won't even see any bats."

"I will come with you. I promise. Now let us talk about something other than bats."

Ryan took Meiling's cold hand and steadied her as the strong wind hit their backs.

The snow had deepened such that they slipped on nearly every step while trying to maintain a brisk pace through the drifting snow. Half of his effort was spent keeping Meiling on her feet.

"I explored all the caves within ten miles of here with my friends when I was ten or eleven. The cave where we're going is over a half-mile long. Without this vicious wind and with the temperature twenty-five degrees warmer, we should be comfortable."

"Can they find your car and then track us to the cave?"

Meiling was obviously trying as hard as possible to keep her mind off the bats. But her question was one that had troubled him since he came up with the plan to hide in the cave.

"We lost them before we left the SUV. Even if they find it after the blizzard conditions end, tracking us to the cave would be nearly impossible unless the wind were to die down much earlier than forecast, leaving our tracks uncovered. I think we're safe for the night."

"What about tomorrow?"

"In the morning, the temperature will be a balmy minus ten. The snow and wind will have stopped, and we will have ten miles or more of visibility. We can see them if they're anywhere nearby. And if they aren't guarding my car, we can drive north toward Redmond, where there are people who can help us."

He pulled Meiling to a stop. "We just started up a hill. This is where the road to the cave branches off to our left. Wait here, Meiling, and please don't move. I need to locate the road and then be able to find my way back to you with near-zero visibility."

She turned her back to the wind and stuck her hands in her coat pockets. "I am not moving until you come back."

In a couple of minutes, Ryan found the road and followed his tracks back to Meiling. "We need to hurry to the road while we can still see my tracks. The wind is swirling around this hill, and it's quickly burying everything with two-foot drifts."

"I am getting cold, Ryan. I need to keep moving, or I will start losing strength."

He took her arm and pulled her to the turn-off for the small dirt road leading to Skeleton Cave. If Meiling was experiencing early symptoms of hypothermia, he needed to get her into the cave and out of the arctic blast, the thief that was stealing her energy.

"Only seven or eight minutes until we reach our tropical paradise."

She nudged him with her shoulder. "Do not you mean our Abaddon?"

"Bats won't destroy you, Meiling, but seriously, Abaddon? Place of destruction. Did you study Hebrew?"

"No. I studied mostly bat viruses."

"A virologist with a phobia about bats. That's got to be situational irony at its best."

"Or at its worst."

He needed to stop the conversation about bats, or he might never get Meiling inside that cave. Maybe he should stop all conversation for a while.

For the next five minutes, the only sounds were the whining of the wind and the crunch of their boots in the snow.

A line of trees appeared—rather, Ryan ran into one of them.

He pulled Meiling to a stop. "Follow me. There's a cliff ahead. We need to circle it. The cave opening is at the bottom."

"So the lava blasted out of the tube and left a hole in the ground? A volcano turned on its side."

"Something like that. We can walk down into the hole from the far side. It's not too steep."

After sliding as much as walking, they reached the bottom. They were out of the arctic blast now, and the air seemed warmer as most of the wind passed over them, leaving a relative calm near the mouth of the cave.

"Let me check the gate. Sometimes it's locked."

The iron bars parted as a small gate swung open. They could enter the cave without Ryan having to shoot a lock off and without risking their pursuers hearing his shot ... or a swarm of bats flying at them.

Meiling followed him into the cave, and Ryan closed the gate behind them.

He took her hand. "Let's go get warm."

"Yes, please. I have never experienced hypothermia before, but I am sure that's what is stealing my strength."

Now that they were safely inside the cave, Ryan turned on the small flashlight he carried in his coat pocket. Rocks of all sizes littered the cave floor.

He carefully picked his way through the rocks. They couldn't afford a sprained ankle tonight.

Once the light came on, Meiling seemed to stay focused on its path as it ran along the cave floor.

He would ensure the light didn't wander upward and reveal the dark creatures that would soon be hanging from the ceiling of the cave.

Nearly ten minutes in, the floor rose several feet, creating a hill. On top of the hill, the air would be warmer.

He led Meiling to the top of the rise and found a flat rock bench lining the left side of the lava tube.

Ryan pointed at the bench.

Meiling scurried toward it.

Ryan's coat was made to be loose-fitting and was a size or two too big. Meiling was slender enough that they could take advantage of the coat's size. "Let me sit first, Meiling. You will sit in front of me with the back of your coat pulled down, so you're sitting on it, not on the cold rock."

He pulled his coat down to his thighs, sat, and scooted his back to the cave wall.

Meiling sat between his knees but gasped when Ryan unzipped his coat and pulled her close to him.

"Pull my coat around you and see if you can zip it up."

She pulled hard on both sides of the coat. "It is about an inch too short."

He circled Meiling's waist with his arms and pulled her snugly against him. "Try it again."

Her fingers fumbled with the zipper for a few seconds. "The zipper started."

"Good. Zip it up as high as it will go."

It stopped a little below her shoulders.

"It is not going to go any farther, Ryan."

Ryan should have anticipated that. He relaxed his hold on her waist. "Now try to relax and squirm into a comfortable position."

She leaned back gently into his chest. "I am comfortable."

"Good. Are you warm?"

"I am warming up. I mean, my body is—I mean—"

"We needed to do this, Meiling, to survive forty-one-degree temperature all night while we're resting."

"Exactly how does this work, I mean physically?"

"Are you asking about the physiology or the physics?"

"Physiology? How could you even think … you know …"

Cuddling up in a cave with a beautiful woman—how could he not think what she was insinuating? "Uh, regarding the physics. By huddling like this, we reduce the surface area of our bodies that's exposed to the environment, and that reduces heat loss."

"That sounds reasonable."

"In meteorology, we spend a lot of time studying thermodynamics. And that's what we have here, a thermodynamic problem. Then there is the other part."

Meiling's body stiffened. "And what part would that be?"

"When a beautiful woman like Dr. Meiling Chen and a red-blooded male like Ryan Adams are forced to spend several hours like this, it reduces heat loss further by generating more—"

"Ryan Adams, how could you?"

"I was only joking, Meiling. It was a poor attempt at humor."

"In this predicament, I cannot turn to see your expression. But you know, Ryan, humor is not funny unless there's an element of truth. So …" she waited.

He didn't reply.

"Well, was it funny or not?"

He didn't reply.

"I know about your Fifth Amendment, Ryan Adams."

Chapter 10

Ryan's joke hinted at a reality he wasn't ready to express to Meiling. It was far too early for that. But the joke ended their conversation for a while.

He relaxed against the cave wall, and Meiling relaxed against him.

Ten minutes later, comfortable warmth had risen to somewhere near hot and sweaty.

He would've asked her if she was getting too warm, but Meiling's deep even breathing said she was sleeping. Given all she had been through over the past four days, exhaustion had probably taken over and demanded rest.

It seemed impossible that the two CCP agents could find them tonight, so Ryan tucked his hands in his coat pockets and slipped into a stupor. Vague thoughts about what tomorrow might bring came, fuzzy but not frightening. Then all thoughts faded away.

Sometime during the night, Meiling tried to turn onto her side. Restrained by his coat, the effort was in vain.

It did, however, wake Ryan. "Are you uncomfortable?"

"I need to move."

"Are you warm enough?"

"Too warm."

"Me too. Unzip my coat and stretch out on the rock bench."

She unzipped the coat.

Ryan quickly zipped it around himself.

Meiling tried to stretch out on the rock and lie down, and then she quickly sat up. "There is no pillow, and the rock is too cold to put my face on."

"But there is a cushy leg about six inches from your head. You should use it as a pillow and try to get some more sleep. You need it."

From the time her head came to rest on his leg until her deep breathing resumed couldn't have been more than a minute.

On the other hand, Ryan got caught in a maze of puzzling plights that he and Meiling might face in the morning. His mind attacked them all with one goal in mind; Meiling must emerge alive and unharmed.

He didn't realize he'd drifted off to sleep again until his cell began playing the Texas Aggie War Hymn, his alma mater's fight song. It served as Ryan's 6:30 a.m. alarm when he wasn't using his radio clock.

By the time he'd silenced the alarm, Meiling had sat up and was busily massaging the muscles in her neck.

"How did you sleep last night?"

"On a rock."

He turned the bright screen of his cell toward her and lit her face.

The smile that stretched the width of her naturally tan face did wonders for his mood.

"I was warm and got some much-needed sleep. You picked a good place for us, Ryan."

"The best place for us now is the cave opening, where we can see if we've been followed."

"But it is still dark."

"In the cave, yes. But by the time we get to the entrance, the twilight will be bright enough to see for a mile or two. In another twenty minutes, we would be able to see all the way to my SUV if it weren't for that small hill blocking our view."

He put his cell away, turned on the flashlight, took Meiling's hand, and pulled her to her feet. "Keep your eyes on the cave floor. There are lava rocks of all sizes. We can't afford any injuries."

She nudged him with her shoulder. "Thanks, Ryan. Rocks beat bats any day ... or night."

"Meiling, these lava tubes have amazing acoustics. They can carry sounds, including human voices, a long, long way. We whisper from now on, and we try not to kick rocks or do anything else that makes noise."

"Do you really think they could have located us here?"

"Not if the storm did its job. But I don't know how long the wind blew before it calmed down. Let's err on the side of caution."

He led Meiling toward the cave entrance a half-mile away, a place where the temperature could be fifty degrees colder, somewhere around ten below. "Keep your hood up, coat zipped, and hands in your pockets," he whispered. "It's about to turn colder, probably colder than anything you've ever experienced."

"What about my hand that seems to have been captured?" Her whisper was soft, barely audible.

"Uh ... like I said, we can't afford you falling and spraining your ankle." He kept her hand.

Two hundred yards ahead, twilight leaked into the cave. In another hundred yards, he turned off the flashlight.

"Can you see the cave floor?"

Meiling nodded.

"Good. Let's keep our talking to an absolute minimum until we determine that we have no visitors."

Forty yards from the entrance, a shadow flickered across the light pouring in through the gate.

Hair bristled on the back of Ryan's neck.

He blocked Meiling with one arm and lifted the back of his coat with the other.

His fingers slid around the grip of his Sig Sauer.

Ryan took a small step ahead and pulled his gun from the holster.

He glanced back at Meiling, a half step back on his left side. Her eyes widened, but she didn't look panicked, only ready to react.

When Ryan focused on the entrance, two shadowy forms now stood outside the gate. The person on the right held what looked like a rifle.

"Down, Meiling."

She dropped to her knees on the floor of the cave.

A red beam from the rifle created a red dot on Meiling's chest.

Ryan dove in front of her.

Hooking her with one arm, he took her down to the cave floor.

A strange belching noise came from some kind of gun.

A sharp sting radiated through his shoulder.

He sat up, raised his weapon, aimed, and returned fire. Three deafening shots cracked in rapid succession and echoed through the cave.

The shooter went down to the ground.

His partner dragged him away from the gate and then supported him as the two stumbled away.

***

The fight was over. The cracking of Ryan's Sig Sauer had left Meiling's ears ringing, and it had started a bat exodus.

Exiting bats now filled the cave.

Meiling should be having a panic attack. But something far more frightening caught her attention and held it.

Ryan reached for his shoulder.

"No, Ryan! Do not touch it."

"Why? Do you know what it is?"

"I think I do. This changes all our plans."

"Meiling, tell me what you're thinking. Don't sugarcoat it. I need to know what we're fighting."

She pulled out a small, plastic sample bag she always kept in her pocket. "Be still. I need to remove the dart."

It came out easily. Maybe it hadn't penetrated his shoulder very deeply after going through his heavy coat. Time would answer that question, but if she was right, time might be in short supply.

Realizing the likely danger to Ryan brought a nauseating knot to Meiling's gut. "Ryan ..." tears overflowed and trickled down her cheeks.

"It's not much of a wound, and it's not your fault. Just give it to me straight. What are we dealing with?"

She took a deep breath and wiped her cheeks. "In the last few weeks that I worked at the Wuhan lab, the military seemed to be playing with NiV, the Nipah Virus. But they did not have the results of my research, so they did not have time to modify the virus. I am almost certain what they shot into you was a strain of NiV currently in the wild in Southeast Asia."

"What does it do, and what is the ... the kill rate?"

"Listen closely. What I am about to tell you means we must get to Dr. Pierce's lab as soon as possible. Three or four hours maximum."

"Meiling, I need a timeline of what to expect."

She blew out a sharp blast of air. "The kill rate for Nipah is ... near seventy-five percent."

He didn't flinch at that shocking news. "How does this disease progress?"

"In the wild, the virus infects through contact with body fluids. It takes a minimum of four days before symptoms appear. But, Ryan, they shot it directly into your bloodstream. Normally, the symptoms progress from fever, headache, a cough, and then to difficulty breathing. After that, the brain is affected so that there's vomiting, confusion, possibly seizures, and then encephalitis. In your case, we will see some difficulty breathing in twenty-four hours and encephalitis in forty-eight hours."

"Wonderful! Sounds like a biowarfare weapon to me."

"I think that was the military's intent if they could use my research to weaponize the Nipah Virus to make it even more effective."

"More effective? This already makes CCP's COVID virus from a few years ago look like a sneeze and some sniffles. So what do we do?"

"We cannot let it progress beyond twenty-four hours if we want to preclude long-term effects."

"Can't let it? Do you mean you can stop it?"

"If I have access to an adequately equipped research lab, my techniques of RNA virus manipulation can, in theory, kill the virus in your body. But I do not know how long that will take. That is why we need your friend, Baker, to fly us to Denver now, and we need to alert Dr. Pierce of our situation and tell him we are coming. I will tell him what resources we will need."

Ryan helped Meiling to her feet and gave her a warm hug. "I trust you, Meiling. You are my best chance, but I'm under no delusion about the seriousness. If you do your best to use your research to accomplish something good, I'm convinced God will bless your efforts." He paused. "Now, Baker said to call if something happened and we needed his help. I think this qualifies. But first, let's see what's happening outside the cave."

As they crept toward the entrance, she noticed the bat migration had stopped. Maybe her phobia about them had ended with a legitimate concern about another person.

She had heard that most mental problems arose from an unhealthy inward focus. Maybe an outward focus on others could cure them.

Meiling shook off thoughts about bats and phobias, and she scanned the sunlit desert, now a glistening white painting dotted with scrubby, snow-coated trees.

Though your sins are like scarlet, they shall be as white as snow; though they are red like crimson, they shall be as wool.

Could that ever be true for Meiling? Ryan could answer that question for her, which was another among a growing list of reasons she had to kill the deadly virus coursing through his bloodstream.

She glanced at Ryan and then sucked in a breath. Instantly, ice coated the inside of her nose. She wrinkled her nose, but it felt almost numb.

Ryan grinned. "Feels weird, doesn't it?"

"Yes, but let us focus on getting ourselves out of here."

She surveyed the area outside the gate. The trail in the snow indicated someone had dragged another person in the snow for a few feet, then helped the injured man walk away from the cave.

The trail continued out of the lava tube's hole in the ground.

Ryan traced the trail with his hand. "Looks like they headed back the way we came in. I'll call Baker, and if he can come, we'll climb out of this hole and wait in the sun."

"How long will it take Baker to get here?"

"If he's near the airport, and the gas tank is full, about fifteen minutes."

"But how—"

"He has a chopper."

"A helicopter?"

"I think I told you that he can fly just about anything with wings ... even if they rotate."

How could Ryan be grinning about her frozen nose and joking when she had just told him he could be dying in a matter of hours. Then his words came to mind.

God will bless your effort.

Ryan trusted her. But if he knew her and all her failings as a Christian, he would not assume God's blessing on her work. That she lived in a Communist country was no excuse. If he lived, maybe Ryan could help her determine what she should do to experience God's blessing.

By the time Meiling ended her musings, Ryan already had Baker on his sat phone, and their lively conversation sounded like it was ending.

Ryan ended the call to Baker. "He's coming in his old military chopper. It's probably not legal to fly that thing in American skies because it still has some military armament."

"How long, Ryan."

"Twenty minutes."

"That is about how long I need to talk to Dr. Pierce to tell him our situation and what I will need to have in the lab. How long will it take to reach the lab?"

"We should be on board the Gulf Stream in an hour, and we'll arrive at the lab after a ninety-minute flight. That should be about three hours from now."

"If Dr. Pierce has the essential equipment and supplies, I can be well into the analysis required to create the Nipah Virus killer in five hours."

"Is that enough time to stop me from dementia or sleeping sickness or whatever you call the brain killer stage?"

"Yes, if we don't encounter any problems. But remember, this is the first actual use of my theories which I have only partly verified in the lab. But I am confident that my theories about the class of RNA viruses are correct."

"And I'm confident too. Come on, Meiling. I told Baker we might check out my car. But we'll have to watch the CCP goons' tracks to ensure they aren't staging an ambush."

"The man you hit looked too seriously wounded to do anything but seek medical attention."

Ryan hooked Meiling's arm. They climbed out of the hole and continued following the tracks of the two men.

They crested the hill in a few minutes, and Ryan's SUV appeared in the distance.

As they drew closer to the vehicle, a set of tire tracks came into view. The tracks made a U-turn in the snow beside the SUV. The CCP agents had left the area.

Ryan pulled her to a stop. "Don't look to your right. I think it's the guy I shot."

"But I—"

"It's not a pretty sight, Meiling."

"Ryan Adams, what letters appear behind my name?"

"Uh ... MD and Ph.D."

"A lot of things you see while becoming an MD are not pretty sights. Let us check him out."

Ryan stopped. "I don't think we need to do that. There's a bullet hole in his forehead, and I didn't make it. I hit him lower, probably in his leg. His buddy murdered him."

Meiling shook her head. "But the CCP would not call it murder. It was a sacrifice made for the greater good."

"I would say for the lesser good," Ryan said. "The dude who shot him knew any medical facility that saw a bullet wound would ask questions and bring in the police."

"So we may still have one man who is trying to kill me?"

"I don't know the CCP and PLA like you do, but I say he's soon going to want to kill the whole crew that's going to Pierce's lab. And I'll bet he has plenty of buddies ready to help. I've heard that these guys are thicker than the old KGB and twice as evil."

She looked beyond Ryan's car. "I hear a helicopter."

"That's Baker's chopper. I'd recognize it anywhere."

"Ryan, I am freezing."

"I was wondering when you would notice that. If you're not from a cold climate, minus ten is brutal."

Baker landed across the road from Ryan's car. The landing created a mini blizzard around the helicopter.

A short, muscular man leaped out and jogged through the snow toward them. "Hey, dude, how are you holding up?"

Meiling took Ryan's hand. "He will be okay for the next twenty-four hours. We have to stop this virus by then."

Baker did a double take on her face and glanced at their clasped hands.

"This is Dr. Meiling Chen. Meiling, meet Radley Baker, a vet and a pilot's pilot."

"We are so thankful you are available to help, Mr. Baker. But please understand that you may also become a target for the CCP."

"That would be nothing new. I've been a target for ISIS, the Taliban, and other groups I'm not allowed to disclose. Might as well add the CCP to the list. Now, let's get you two to the Redmond Airport. The Gulf Stream is being fueled as we speak."

"Ryan, I forgot that I left something at your house."

"Not a problem," Baker said. "I'll set down in the field across the street from his house. Ryan can run in and grab it, and we'll be on our way in two minutes."

Meiling studied Ryan for a moment. "You're not running anywhere. We don't need your heart pumping NiV through your body any faster than it already is."

The three climbed into the helicopter and buckled in.

The engine revved, and Meiling's stomach flip-flopped when the chopper leaped up into the air and turned.

Two minutes later, Baker landed across the street from Ryan's home.

Meiling's heart raced as she looked at the house.

The front door stood open, and there were large tire tracks along the street in front of the house.

"Adams, it looks like you had a visitor," Baker said.

"I won't run, Meiling, but I need to enter first and make sure there are no surprises." Ryan already had his gun in hand.

Once again, they were wasting precious moments.

Please, God. Protect Ryan and give us the time we need.

Chapter 11

January 5, 12:30 a.m., Rocky Mountain Metro

Almost four hours had elapsed since Ryan's infection by the dart. Meiling had only forty-four hours left until the Nipah Virus won the battle and twenty hours until Ryan became gravely ill.

Her ears throbbed as Baker completed a rapid descent to the Rocky Mountain Metro runway.

The clock was ticking, and the thought of the challenges still ahead brought the knot back to Meiling's gut.

After the Gulfstream landed and started taxiing toward a building on their right, she focused her attention on Ryan sitting in the seat beside her.

"Ryan, do you feel any symptoms yet—headache or—" She laid her hand against his forehead. "You do not feel warm."

Ryan met her gaze, and there was a softness in his eyes that she had seen often since she met him. "Maybe I shouldn't tell you how I feel."

"This is not a time for joking or for ..." She didn't complete her thought.

"I'm going to tell you anyway, and I'm not joking. I'm in the care of the world's foremost authority on RNA viruses like NiV. I trust her and she trusts God. For someone in my position, it doesn't get any better than that."

"So I am caring for an optimist." But his optimism did not infect her with Ryan's confidence. It only increased the pressure on someone who had a tenuous relationship with God. However, this was not the time to raise that issue. But

75

that time would eventually come, and it could destroy everything Meiling had found in America.

Ryan grinned. "So I'm not supposed to be an optimist. Would you prefer I have a nervous breakdown or maybe a panic attack?"

"I would prefer that you be still, relax, let me brief Dr. Pierce and find out if we have everything we need in his lab."

Baker's voice came through the sound system. "I see Pierce's van near where we'll be parking. Since there are no snowstorms, ice storms, or damaging winds forecast for the next week, my Gulfstream will be safe sitting on the tarmac. I'll stick around for two or three days until you're settled in. If you need a fast getaway, I'll be available."

After Baker parked and lowered the steps, Meiling hurried down them to meet Dr. Pierce.

Pierce was a middle-aged man of medium height. Wearing a western leather coat and jeans, he certainly was not putting on airs.

"Dr. Pierce, I am Meiling Chen."

He extended a hand, and she shook it.

"It's good to meet you, Dr. Chen. Just call me Robert."

"And I am just Meiling."

Ryan caught up with Meiling and stood beside her. "Can I shake hands, or should I refrain from that?"

Meiling looked his way. "Until we know more about your virus, you should refrain."

"But Meiling, most of the way here you were holding my—"

"Doctor's privilege, Ryan." She turned to Robert. "I need to brief you on our situation and do a quick inventory of your lab equipment."

"Then let's all climb in the van. We can talk while my driver takes us to the facility."

Two minutes later, the driver sped away from the airport while she gathered her thoughts about how to best describe their situation.

Robert stroked his short beard. "Meiling, would you please refresh my memory about how the Nipah Virus infects and gets to the central nervous system?"

This was a good place to start, and Robert evidently knew that. "Yes, of course." She paused for a moment. "Sometimes NiV goes through the nasal turbinates to the olfactory bulb and on to the brain. But in Ryan's case, a dart had injected it, so the virus will take a hematogenous route, that is, through the bloodstream. Viral replication in the cerebrovascular endothelial cells will likely disrupt the blood-brain barrier, and the Nipah Virus will enter his central nervous system. This causes the onset of the most serious Nipah symptoms, seizures, encephalitis, and coma. And that is what we must prevent if Ryan is to recover fully." She paused.

Robert needed to know about their critical time constraints, so Meiling continued. "We are four hours into a forty-eight-hour race to our deadline. In about twenty hours, Ryan will become symptomatic. Twenty-four hours after that, he could be in a coma.

"I see."

"In your latest interview with Ryan, you indicated you were investigating how we might get several different types of proteins into our bodies. So I assume you can make a lipid nanoparticle (LNP) delivery system."

"Yes. Once we came to understand the interaction of molecules—"

"You mean the interaction of lipids, proteins, and nucleotides?"

"That is correct, and understanding those interactions, we have now streamlined the creation of the LNPs for delivery of mRNA. We can create the needed LNP in a matter of hours."

"Five or six hours?"

"Yes, if there are no problems with the equipment in the lab."

"About my requirements for lab equipment. The NiV is a nonsegmented, single-stranded, negative-sense RNA virus. I understand the RNA of the virus, but to be certain of what we're dealing with, ideally, I would have mNGS—uh … metagenomic, next-generation sequencing capability for determination of microbial DNA and RNA sequences."

"My lab has mNGS capability for determining sequences."

"But to do my work, I must peer deeper into the sequences. I need an electron microscope that can image to a resolution of the width of the hydrogen atom."

"My electron microscopes provide close to that resolution. We'll have to pray it's enough."

"Then we will pray. If I can see what I need to, that will give me the info needed to create a small piece of RNA called a probe. As you probably know, the probe is designed to have a complementary sequence to the target RNA sequence. At this point, based on my research, I need to modify a portion of the probe's molecule that will cause it to bind to the target RNA."

"What does the binding accomplish?"

"The target RNA is destroyed."

"But how—"

"Please trust me on this, Dr. Pierce. It will be destroyed."

"I trust you. But I see a huge problem. How do you produce and distribute the probe in sufficient quantities to stop the infection?"

"We have only one option if we want to save Ryan's life. We wrap up the mRNA in a lipid nanoparticle (LNP) and use the cells of his body to manufacture enough probes to kill the virus. Nipah loves to race through the bloodstream, and it's there that we must stop it. But if Ryan cannot produce enough probes, I will also infect my body with the mRNA particles. We can examine Ryan's and my concentrations of the probe. If I am producing more than Ryan, we draw blood from him and then replace it with mine. When NiV is no longer active in his body, the process stops, and Ryan's body cleans up everything except the probe mRNA."

"But what about you, Meiling?"

She grinned. "Make sure you leave me enough blood to survive."

His face looked like it might turn green.

"Dr. Pierce, are you comfortable giving IVs and transfusions?"

"Capable, yes. Comfortable, we'll see. But Meiling, how do I shut down the probe factories that will be running inside both of you?"

"Hopefully, I will feel well enough to do it. The kidneys will do their part, but they will need help. Like for a coronavirus, we can use zinc and a zinc ionophore such as hydroxychloroquine, quercetin, or EGCG. Quercetin is preferable because we can get it at local health food stores. But you must give the solution to us through an IV. This will stop mRNA replication and reduce the concentration of the nanoparticles in our blood. Keep administering them until you see that our blood reaches a threshold level of nanoparticles that I will specify. It might take a few hours."

"What concentrations do we need in the IV?"

"It depends on the particular zinc ionophore we are using. We will look up what the doctors recommended who performed early treatment of COVID-19 back in the SARS-CoV-2 days. Those concentrations are documented and should work fine because we will be doing the same thing those doctors were doing."

Robert's bushy eyebrows pinched. "But we're talking about performing transfusions. What about your blood types?"

Meiling smiled. "I already asked him about that. Ryan and I are a perfect match."

Chapter 12

January 4, 11:00 p.m. Pacific Time, Redmond, Oregon

Tao Huang sat in his rented four-wheel-drive vehicle outside the Redmond Municipal Airport. Calling his contact and supervisor, Zhang Hu, would be unpleasant and possibly punitive, but he had lost his two targets near the cave, where he had also lost his comrade. He had no other option but to call in his status.

He punched in Hu's number on his secure phone and waited for an explosion.

"This is Hu."

"This is Tao Huang."

"Do you have Dr. Chen?"

"No."

"You did not kill her, did you?"

"No. We did not kill her, and the dart will not kill her for at least two more days."

"Tell me what happened, and it must include Chen's status."

"She was hiding in a cave with an American. She escaped. But we had our laser beam on her when we fired, so I believe Dr. Chen was hit by the dart."

"Hiding in a cave? So she escaped, and she has an American accomplice? This is not helpful, Huang. She could still give the Americans her research results before she dies."

"The man she was with, Ryan Adams, opened fire on us. We did not know he had a gun."

"You fool!" Hu's words blasted through the phone. Huang pulled the cell from his ear. "You are in Oregon on the eastern side of the state. Everybody there has a gun."

"Zheng was hit. He did not make it."

Tao waited for another furious blast from Hu, but he did not reply.

"I immediately left the cave for Adams' house because the two were obviously together. But I found nothing of value. Either her data is on her, or she has hidden it." Tao paused.

Still no response.

"I had to leave at that point because an old military helicopter with weapons approached. It landed at Adams' house. Adams went inside and got something. Then the helicopter left. It headed north toward the local airport."

"Are you saying the U.S. military is now involved?"

"No, Hu. The helicopter was too old to still be in service. But I went to the airport, looked around, and found the helicopter. Airport maintenance workers told me the owner is Radley Baker, a military veteran who owns two aircraft based at the Redmond Airport. The other aircraft, a Gulfstream 550, was gone. I guess we lost them."

"You idiot." The words came in a growling accusation. With Comrade Hu, this was where conversations either got better or much, much worse.

"**You** may have lost them, Huang, but **they** are not lost. Use our contact in the FAA. With the name, aircraft model, and pilot's city of residence, he should be able to look up the plane. When you get its identifying information, use the tracking system to look up that plane's most recent flight plan. Then you are back on the trail. Huang, I should not have to do your job for you. Do you understand?"

"They are aware of our pursuit now. So after I locate them, I will need more help to take Dr. Chen."

"You were supposed to use the dart as you were capturing Dr. Chen and then promise to give her antibodies if she would give us her data. But now she is running loose, the antibodies do not exist, and you only have, at best, forty-eight hours to find her before encephalitis sets in. If that happens, we lose everything Chen discovered at the Wuhan lab. And you, Huang, will lose your rank and perhaps a lot more."

Hu paused. "Call me as soon as you determine your requirements, and I will find others to help."

"If Chen is alive when I find her, she will be sick. We have no antibodies or vaccines. If I touch her, I might—"

"Use your imagination. You must solve the problems you encounter, Huang. You must tear the place apart, torture its occupants, and do anything necessary to locate her research data. That data is critical to our plan to end American dominance. If you fail, you may set our efforts back several years. That would not be good for your career. It would not be good for you personally, Huang."

"And what about Mr. Adams, the pilot, and others who may know about Dr. Chen's work and her defection?"

"Capture them, interrogate them, then kill them all."

"But—"

"Do what our Nike friends say. Just do it, Huang."

Chapter 13

January 5, 2:30 a.m., Dr. Pierce's lab outside of Superior, Colorado

When Robert set up an account for Meiling on his server, she took care of their highest priority, copying her research data to a directory on the server.

"Robert, my data is on the server, under my account. You have the password for it. It's in a directory called RNA_viruses, located under my home directory. In that directory, you will find an index.html file. It is the top-level index for the documentation of my data. Each subdirectory contains an HTML file explaining the contents of the directory and containing links deeper into the data directories. All HTML files have links back up to the index file." She paused.

"You can navigate all the documentation with a web browser. For me, the data seems completely documented, but no one else has used it, so you can tell me what you think about its utility."

"Meiling, you are already far ahead of most of the data brought to my lab. I locked up in my safe my copy of the micro-SD cards you made for me."

"So we have a copy of my research results on your server and in your safe. That will do for now. But we cannot trust anyone else with the data."

"You're right. But we will have to cross that bridge at the appropriate time."

Meiling nodded. "I am going to check on Ryan, and then we can get started analyzing the contents of the dart I pulled from his shoulder."

She turned to leave the room, then stopped. "Robert, you might want to look up the directory that I named RNA_virus_commonalities and read its documentation. That is what we will be focusing on initially. It provides our key to unlocking the Nipah Virus, not all the details, just the basic principles involved."

There was something else she needed to know. What was it? "Oh, I do have a question about creating the liquid nanoparticles, the LNPs that we will need to encapsulate the mRNA. What equipment do you have, and how long will it take to make, say ... a liter of LNPs?"

"I bought some specially fabricated equipment when I could get it cheaply after the COVID pandemic. It does microfluidic formulation of LNPs. That's a technique we can easily scale up to the production level you require."

"How many devices do you have?"

"Two that are usable. Don't worry. We can make more nanoparticles in an hour than Ryan can take over all the time we have left."

They had set up a temporary bed for Ryan in the BSL-3 area and had tried to make it as comfortable as possible. They weren't following BSL-3 procedures because Pierce had no pathogens in that lab, and Ryan was not contagious at this stage. When he became symptomatic, or they started working on him, he would need to be in the BSL-4 facility that Robert built last year. It would not be comfortable, Ryan would be sick then, and they would be poking and prodding him.

When Meiling entered, Ryan had the hospital-type bed raised to sit and his hands clasped behind his head.

She pulled one of his hands out and wrapped both of hers around it. "How are you feeling?"

"Meiling, are you supposed to be doing that? I'm contaminated."

"I doubt that you're contagious yet, and I will wash my hands after I leave. Now, has anything changed in the way you feel?"

"Yes, I'm bored."

"I meant anything physically different in how you feel."

He scanned her face and grinned. "Now that *you* came in, I feel—"

"You are impossible. Do you have any Nipah symptoms? Any at all?"

"No."

"That is good. We do not want to see any symptoms before seven o'clock this morning."

"We're on mountain time here. That would be nine o'clock this morning, which would be in five or six more boring hours."

"People do not usually catch Nipah Virus by injection. So my estimates of incubation time and symptom onset were only educated guesses."

"I'll bet those biowarfare guys in Wuhan know how long it takes. They probably injected some people to make sure their little dart worked. Isn't that how the CCP does things in China?"

"Yes. But I do not want to think about that. I need to concentrate on getting you well."

The soft look filled his eyes again. So inviting and trusting.

Tears welled and threatened to run down her cheeks. She pulled her hand from Ryan's and brushed the tears from her eyes.

"Meiling, look what you did with an unwashed, contaminated hand. You wiped your eye. You need to be more careful. I'm a biological weapon. I'm not safe."

"I am a doctor, and I can take care of myself. I can take care of you too, Ryan Adams. I am going to keep you alive and safe if it is the last thing I do."

"If you do to yourself some of those things you described to Pierce, it very well could be the last thing you do. Don't take chances with your life, Meiling. Not on my account."

She was becoming convinced that being with Ryan, and talking to him, gave value to her life. Without him, could it ever have value again? And Ryan was the one person who could answer her questions about her standing with her Heavenly Father.

Meiling should have spent more time studying her Bible, but that had, been nearly impossible in Wuhan with its secrets and surveillance.

She needed to leave now before her emotions interfered with the work she must do. "I will be back no later than five o'clock to check on you."

When she dropped his hand, he clamped it to his forehead.

"Wow. That was almost a knockout punch."

"Is your head hurting?"

"It feels like somebody just started pounding on my head with a rubber mallet."

This could not be happening. It was far too early. Regardless, it was time to press the accelerator to the floor for their operations in the lab.

"Ryan, we can bring you something for your headache in a few minutes. But first, Robert and I need to move you to the BSL-4 lab to maintain containment. Things will be much more intense in there for the next twenty-four hours. I am praying for you, Ryan. I—I ..." She turned to leave the room before he could see that she was crying.

"And I'm praying for you too, Meiling."

Chapter 14

January 5, 9:00 a.m., 15 hours until NiV breaches Ryan's blood-brain barrier

The door to the level three lab opened, and one of Pierce's lab workers came in wearing strange-looking protective gear that was far short of the moon suits Ryan expected to see.

"Mr. Adams, it's time to take you to the level four lab. Things may seem a bit strange in there, but that's mostly for our protection so we can effectively protect you. Any questions?"

Oh, he had questions like, how much will this hurt? Can I talk to Meiling while she's inside one of those moonwalk suits? What are the odds I will leave the lab alive? But they were not appropriate, especially for people trying so hard to save his life.

"No questions. Let's get this show on the road. Wait a minute. Will I be able to talk with anyone while they're inside a, what is it, a positive pressure suit?"

"They will have radios in their suits for communication. You will have a radio too, but unless you are in a conscious state where you can use it, you won't be able to communicate."

If possible, Meiling would make sure he could talk to them. Knowing her as he did put that concern to rest. How much things would hurt, and questions about coming out alive would have to wait for answers.

Now the rubber mallet seemed to have turned into a ball peen hammer. When were they going to bring him something for his headache?

The level 3 lab was not hosting any pathogens, so the lab worker simply pushed him through a couple of doors and out of the lab. But looming a few yards ahead was an ominous-looking door.

"Mr. Adams, inside the door ahead is an airlock that will prevent any air exchange from the lab to us. I will push you into the airlock and shut the door. You may hear rushing air for a short time, then the other door will open, and they will take you into the level 4 lab. Any questions?"

The airlock would be no problem. Whatever pain and anguish he would experience lay beyond the second door.

"No questions. Let's go."

His bed rolled into the airlock.

After the whooshing of air, the level 4 lab door opened, and he saw Meiling's face through the plastic-like face covering.

She smiled, and the thumb on her glove pointed upward.

He returned the thumb-up that expressed more confidence than Ryan felt. But just seeing her face drove the pain of his headache down to a more tolerable level.

Robert handed him a small two-way radio and immediately inserted an IV needle in his left arm.

Meiling placed his radio on his stomach and drew blood from his right arm. She took it to her workbench and examined it using a tall, strange-looking microscope.

A few minutes later, Meiling's voice came over the radio. "As we expected, the virus in your blood matches that in the dart. But I couldn't afford to risk making the wrong probe. I'm starting to assemble the probe now. But be patient. It will take a while."

Soon Ryan's headache returned with a vengeance. Now his throat became scratchy, and he developed a cough. He didn't want to think about what came next on the time-ordered list of symptoms. But it was hard not to think about the symptom termed **difficulty breathing**.

To take his mind off the life-threatening symptoms which were approaching, he studied Meiling as she worked.

She alternated between the funny-looking microscope and the sequencing device. But she concentrated so intently that it was impossible to read anything into her body language or the occasional glimpses of her face through the transparent face covering.

Robert entered the airlock and returned with water and a bottle of an OTC pain reliever. He dumped three pills in Ryan's hand.

He gladly swallowed them.

The headache subsided in another thirty minutes, and he dozed intermittently.

When he awoke, Ryan could see the screensaver on one of the laptops. The time displayed on it said five minutes until noon, nearly nine hours since the onset of symptoms.

Only about fifteen hours remained until the Nipah zombies went after his brain.

Meiling swiveled in her chair and faced him.

Robert rolled his chair over to join them.

"I have gotten the probe's sequence, and I see what I need to do to modify it so it will destroy the Nipah RNA upon binding with it. Once we modify the probe, we need to create the mRNA that will reproduce the killer probe and then turn it loose in Ryan's body and mine. We will need another bed here, Robert, so you can draw my blood as needed. Can we make enough room?"

"I've got a smaller bed stored away. But we won't be putting it in here."

Meiling's face took on that fierce look Ryan had only seen a couple of times. Then it relaxed.

"The problem is …" Meiling paused. "The work I have outlined will take at least twenty-four hours, and we have only fifteen hours left."

"So the Nipah zombies will have a nine-hour feast before we assassinate them?" Ryan said.

"No. We cannot let that happen," Meiling said. "We will start by trying to stretch fifteen hours to twenty-four."

"What are you proposing?" Robert said.

"Studies show that both copper and zinc can slow NiV replication within cells. But if both are present, the ratio of one to the other impacts the effectiveness of controlling replication. We do not have time to determine the optimum ratio."

Robert stroked his beard and then looked up at Meiling. "So, how do you want to approach the problem."

"I propose that we select zinc alone since we already have it in stock. And we use quercetin for our zinc ionophore. Your lab worker already got us a good supply from a local health food store. We will give Ryan zinc and quercetin intravenously at the maximum dosage recommended by frontline doctors during the COVID-19 pandemic."

"In theory," Robert said, "we should see a reduction or a slowing in the rate of increase of NiV in his blood."

"Exactly, but I do not know how much we can slow it down. By now, Ryan's body is mounting an immune response against the virus too. We must pray that together the two are enough."

"I'm on it," Robert said. "I'll look up that max concentration too."

Behind the positive pressure suit's face covering, Meiling's head nodded. "Back to modifying the probe." She turned toward her lab workbench. "And, unless something important happens that we need to talk about, we must be quiet in here. I need to concentrate, and I cannot afford any time to recover from a mistake."

Ryan would pray that there would be no mistakes, both for his sake and for the woman he was developing deep feelings for.

Chapter 15

January 5, 9:15 a.m. Outside Dr. Pierce's lab

Tao Huang crept through the trees and scrubby bushes lining a small stream called Coal Creek.

A thick layer of clouds had formed, diminishing the light. That may help to hide his approach.

The line of trees by the creek widened near the perimeter of the lab, forming a small forest of mostly deciduous trees. Unfortunately, it was January, and there were no dense leaves to hide him. However, there were many thick tree trunks, enough to hide a slender man trying to assess the strength of the security around the facility.

There were sensors mounted on the building, which lay a hundred yards away.

Tao pulled his binoculars to his eyes and focused. Motion sensors and video cameras appeared evenly spaced along the sides of the building. A third device looked like it could shoot a projectile up to three or four inches in diameter. But those were probably sirens.

So far, Tao had only seen one person outside the lab, a short, muscular man who had walked the perimeter about fifty yards out from the lab.

Was he doing routine surveillance, or did they expect an attack? Regardless, it made Tao's task more difficult, and he needed more help.

He called his superior, Zhang Hu.

"This is Hu."

"This is Tao Huang. I have just evaluated the lab where Dr. Chen is hiding, infected with Nipah. To get to her, we need at least three more men, some RPGs, and both anti-tank and anti-personnel grenades. The men must bring their own rifles and ammunition."

"Why not ask for a tank and close air support from a JH-7 and perhaps a Z-9 attack helicopter?"

"But these are the requirements I need for—"

"Huang, contact these two men, Ming Guo and Yong Lu. They are within your sector. I will text you their contact information. You can have them and whatever resources they have. Take what you have, plan accordingly, capture Dr. Chen, and get her research data. As I said before, just do it, Huang."

Hu ended the call.

The contact information for the two men came a few minutes later.

Tao called Ming Gao the most senior of the two men.

"This is Ming."

"Ming, my name is Tao Huang. I'm on a mission under the command of Zhang Hu."

"He told us you would call. Where exactly are you?"

"I am on the southwest side of Superior, a little northwest of Denver. You can get in the vicinity by driving West Coal Creek Drive from Superior. I am about two kilometers southwest of Superior."

"Good. That is not far from Yong Lu and me. What is the time frame?"

"We must complete the mission in less than twenty-four hours, ideally by midnight tonight. I need you to bring your military rifles and ammunition, an RPG launcher, and three rounds of anti-tank and anti-personnel grenades."

"Huang, this is not China. It is America. I will bring what we have, our rifles and ammo, a grenade launcher, and four grenades."

"What type of grenades?"

"We have two anti-tank grenades, one anti-personnel grenade, and another grenade that is different. Maybe an HEDP."

The biggest problem was that Tao needed to extract Dr. Chen alive to find her research data, so he could not go in with RPGs and blow the place up. And with limited anti-personnel grenades, they would have to rely mostly on rifles to take out any men on the ground. That could make the mission longer and much more dangerous.

On the other hand, if things got too hot, he would go in with anti-tank RPGs and blow up the biosafety labs, incinerating the virus. At least he would be alive.

Chapter 16

January 5, 9:30 a.m.

Radley Baker drove the Jeep SUV he rented at the airport to Pierce's lab. After visiting the lab and walking the perimeter, he had a few concerns about people with evil intent getting too close or breaching the lab if they were a trained assault team.

The best way to bolster security was to add people outside the current security perimeter to detect or engage any threat that came into the area.

One body wasn't enough to cover the half-mile outer perimeter of the present lab security zone. He needed at least three more people he could trust, one on each side of the lab.

If he remembered correctly, four members of his old combat team lived in the area from Colorado Springs up to Boulder, all within a ninety-minute drive of Superior. Could he snag three of them? There was only one way to find out.

He kept the team member's numbers in a special place in his contact list. After ten years, cell numbers and people might have changed. But remembering those men as he did, Baker would bet that not all of them had changed, not in the ways that really mattered. And their patriotism was unquestionable.

He chose three to call, Rafer Jackson, Randy Beamon, and Vance Nelson.

He hit Rafer's number in his contacts.

"This can't be Radley Baker, can it?"

"Yeah. It's me. How're you doing, Rafe?"

"Doing good. Got me a wife and a six-year-old son. How about you, Rad?"

"I've got a wife and twin daughters. And I **was** doing good until something cropped up yesterday. Tell me, Rafe, what do you think about China and the CCP."

"Talk about changing the subject. Well, I try not to use the language it would take to describe that power-mongering, murderous bunch of thieves and racists."

"That answers my question. Now I've got a story to tell you. After you hear it, I need to know if you can help on a little mission I've got planned."

Baker told Rafer Meiling's and Ryan's story and their current critical situation at Dr. Pierce's lab. "Rafe, I'm concerned that CCP agents may locate them as early as tonight if they can find out about my involvement and check my flight plan to the airport. Would you be willing to dedicate the next week to watching the perimeter of the lab's security system with me?"

"Watching? It might come to a lot more than that. I still have the M4 I snagged in that wonky withdrawal from Afghanistan. I couldn't let the Taliban have my gun."

"That sounds great, Rafe. I plan to call Randy and Vance too. That would give us a man on each side of the lab."

"Good call, bro. Randy's got an Afghan souvenir, too, something he really shouldn't have but which could come in handy if the lab comes under assault. Don't know how he got it shipped home."

"Don't tell me that crazy pyromaniac has a grenade launcher?"

"Yep. An M203. And he managed to get three or four grenades, M433s or M406s. We gave away so much sophisticated weaponry to the Taliban that we thought it only right to deplete their stock as much as we could. We were so angry about the whole mess that we were willing to take chances."

Baker chuckled. "We're going to be so illegal. But if we stop the Commies and give Meiling and Pierce time to do their work on Ryan, it's more than worth the risk."

"Let me know how it goes with Randy and Vance."

"Will do. I plan to have a conference call to coordinate us linking up and finalizing our defense strategy."

"Baker, I'll be waiting for that call."

He ended the call with Rafer and looked up Randy's number.

Fifteen minutes later, Baker had commitments to help from the other two men, Randy and Vance. Each said they would bring their most powerful weaponry.

As he set up the conference call for the four of them, Baker prayed that he could deploy his team of four around the lab before the CCP showed up. Otherwise, they could lose the lab and everyone in it.

Chapter 17

January 5, 3:00 p.m., ten hours until Ryan's symptoms turn severe

Meiling had made a lot of killer probes in the past five hours, and Robert had placed the probes and the LNP he had created into his microfluidic formulation process.

By 3:15 p.m., they had enough nanoparticles to start injecting them into both Meiling and Ryan so their bodies could begin manufacturing the killer probes, hopefully in quantities great enough to kill the Nipah Virus infecting Ryan. Or, in Meiling's case, to outproduce Ryan, so her blood would be rich enough to give it to Ryan to increase his quantity of Nipah-killing probes.

Right now, the most crucial battle they were fighting in Ryan's body was the battle of the blood-brain barrier, the brain's microvascular endothelial cells. This thin lining of cells in the blood vessels near his brain acted as a shield against pathogens like NiV.

If the concentration of NiV rose too high, the virus would cause excessive endothelial cell damage. NiV would then leave the blood vessels, breaking the blood-brain barrier and giving NiV a free shot at Ryan's central nervous system, his brain. Then, as Ryan quipped, the Nipah zombies would start eating his brain—a gruesome, graphic analogy but one that represented reality.

Robert turned toward Meiling. "Young lady, it's time for you to move back to the level 3 lab so I can get to your bare arm with this needle."

That would never work. She would be moving back and forth between labs, disinfecting, then suiting up again. They would lose too much time, and that would cost Ryan his life. But if she objected, Robert would insist that she follow the protocols.

There is only one way to make this work.

Meiling unfastened her head covering and began pulling it off.

"Meiling, no!" Robert's rigid body sagged into resignation when he realized she was already exposed to the deadly pathogen Ryan had brought into the level 4 lab.

She continued to take her suit off. It did not really matter. In a few moments, Meiling would be injected with the nanoparticles that would protect her from the Nipah Virus. If they did not work, she and Ryan could die together, and Dr. Pierce could continue her work to find a probe that would kill NiV.

Ryan stared at her, wide-eyed, disbelieving.

She grinned at him. "It is okay, Ryan. You and I are about to get vaccinated. Nipah is about to get nipped."

She turned toward Robert. "Now we can do injections and transfusions with no delays. Prepare the syringes, Robert. We are ready."

The lab clock now read five minutes until six o'clock. At 4:20 p.m., 4:50 p.m., 5:20 p.m., and 5:50 p.m., Robert had injected both Ryan and Meiling with the nanoparticles.

There were only seven hours left to save Ryan's life. Meiling needed to know if her rapidly kludged system had made sufficient progress. But they must wait another hour to see the impact of the last injection.

"Robert, would you please draw blood samples from Ryan and me at seven o'clock? We need to check his blood for levels of the probe and NiV and mine for probe levels."

"Will do. Last time, your probe level was fifty percent ahead of Ryan. But I'm also going to check your NiV levels,

Meiling. Since that little stunt with your PP suit, you are vulnerable to infection. How are you feeling?"

"Like I gave a pint of blood two hours ago. But I drank a glass of orange juice."

"Any dizziness?"

"No. Now that my blood sugar is up a bit, I am fine."

"Any headache?"

"No, Robert. I really am fine."

At seven o'clock, Robert brought in two syringes and prepared to draw blood from the two.

"Me first," Meiling said, wanting to give Ryan another couple of minutes—anything for his body to produce more NiV-killing probes before they checked it.

After Robert drew blood from both, he took the samples to a microscope at the far end of the workbench from where Meiling and Ryan lay.

At 7:30 p.m., he approached with a heavily scribbled piece of paper.

"Tell me some good news, Robert."

"The good news is that Ryan is at ninety percent of the target level of your killer probes. But the bad news is that we need at least another fifteen percent reduction in the NiV levels. Then we can be reasonably sure that we have stopped the increase of NiV and are winning the battle."

"Then we must give him more of my blood."

"Meiling, I won't do that."

"You have to, Robert. We cannot let it end like this, not when we are so close to stopping the spread of his Nipah infection."

"I just took a pint of your blood not even three hours ago."

"Yes, you took ten percent of my blood. If you take another pint, it still doesn't send me into hypovolemic shock. Do it, Robert!"

"Young lady, you're going to have to compromise on this issue. We can't afford to lose you." Robert blew out a sharp blast of air. "Here's the deal. I will draw another half pint of your blood at a few minutes before ten o'clock. No more, so don't ask. If we transfuse it into Ryan by a few minutes after ten, that just might cut off the growth of the NiV infection before 1:00 a.m."

"I would give him all my blood if I knew that would stop the virus."

Ryan's head swiveled toward her and met her gaze. He had heard her remark.

Meiling sat up on the side of her bed. The room seemed to rock back and forth.

Ryan's strong hand clasped her shoulder. "Whoa, Meiling." His voice was hoarse. "You're not ready for anything but to rest and take in some more fluids."

Robert and Ryan were both right. But it brought a level of frustration she had never before experienced.

Meiling leaned back against the partially raised head of her bed and rolled onto her side to face Ryan.

He gave her a weak smile. "And I appreciate your willingness to sacrifice yourself for me. But that's not going to happen, Meiling. Right now, the world and this nation need you a lot more than they need me. You'll see when this crisis ends. You will have saved my life without having to sacrifice yours."

"But how can you know that, Ryan?"

"You wouldn't believe me if I told you."

Beads of sweat covered his forehead, and he seemed to be struggling to string words together.

"And I really don't feel like fighting you right now, Meiling. But I'm with Dr. Pierce on this one. I'm not ready for more blood yet, and you're not giving me any of yours except as Robert specified."

Ryan reached out with his free and cupped her cheek. "It's going to be okay. You've already done more than anyone on this planet could have done. Let's finish this right and let God give us His outcome."

Ryan's hand slid from her cheek down her arm and took her hand. "I've got to lie down for a bit. You probably should too." He leaned back on his pillow but kept her hand.

But her hand was not all that Ryan kept. He may not know it, but he also had a huge chunk of her heart. She would gladly give it all to him if it were not for the barrier that remained, the compromising life that she had led in Wuhan. She had excuses, excuses that many people would probably accept. But a holy and righteous God would never accept them. She still needed to talk to Ryan about that. But for that to happen, Ryan Adams must win his battle with the Nipah Virus.

Chapter 18

January 5, 10:20 p.m., along Coal Creek near Dr. Pierce's lab

Tao Huang peered through the trees using his SVG Night Vision Goggles. "We need to attack full force now before they can react. Ming, is the RPG ready?"

"Yes, but it is loaded with the HEAT warhead," Ming Guo said.

"Anti-tank?"

"Yes. Is that a problem?"

"Think about it, Ming. This is a BSL-3 lab, and according to intelligence, it likely has a level 4 lab, too. They have Nipah Virus inside, and you are planning to hit it with a round that will penetrate and blow everything inside to who knows where. One shot could infect all of us, you, me, and Yong Lu too."

"But what if I do not hit the lab?"

"You had better not hit the lab. Shoot for the right side of the building, where there are some windows. There will not be any lab where there are windows."

"How does that help our attack?

"If there are any sentries, they will rush to the point of attack. Then we take them out and enter the building. If there are no sentries, we enter immediately."

Yong took a step closer to Tao. "How do you plan to capture an infected Dr. Chen?"

"Don't touch her, and we will not be infected."

Yong shifted his feet and stared at the ground. "Tao, she is going to be inside a level four lab, and she *is* infected. Who is going in to get her out?"

Yong had driven the point home, a point Tao should have understood from his last phone conversation with Zhang Hu. ***This was a suicide mission.*** Though he had not realized it, this had been a suicide mission from the moment that Chen and the man got away from Redmond because Chen would be contagious before they could track her down.

Tao was, as Zhang Hu had called him, a fool.

At a minimum, someone would have to blow the doors off the level 4 lab, which could infect them. Then they would have to capture Dr. Chen and interrogate her. That would surely infect whoever entered the lab.

There was only one solution that made any sense and kept Tao alive. They must locate the level 4 lab and, from outside the building, use the last two high-explosive anti-tank (HEAT) warheads to incinerate the lab. The intense heat should destroy the virus too. Then he could tell Hu what happened, say it was their only option, insist that a copy of Dr. Chen's research data was somewhere in the lab outside the biosafety areas, and convince Hu that Tao would find it.

Hu would be furious. But it sounded reasonable that the data would not be in the protected lab rooms. Dr. Pierce and Chen could not use her information until it was on one of the servers, and the servers would certainly not be in a biosafety area.

Maybe Tao would be fortunate, find the data, and placate Hu. If not, Tao would have to flee somewhere to hide or find asylum. But ***somewhere*** did not include the United States of America—not after the attack which he would have just led against an American lab and those inside it.

"Ming, Yong, listen closely. This is what we will do to satisfy our superiors ... and to stay alive.

"We will move one hundred meters to our right and launch a round into the building near the windows. That gives us a way to enter Dr. Pierce's facility. Yong will run inside the building and find the BSL-4 lab location. Ming and I will wait to see if any sentries approach us. If so, we take them out.

"When Yong returns, we will move back to this spot and launch two anti-tank warheads into the side of the building at the level 4 lab location that Yong has validated. The HEAT warheads should incinerate the virus and the people in the lab."

"But that—"

"Let me finish. I will convince Hu that Dr. Chen's research data is in the lab, on a server outside of the biosafety areas, and I will tell him we will find and retrieve it."

Yong stiffened and met his gaze. "And if we do not find it?"

"Then we are all on our own to find a new homeland."

"You traitor." Yong shifted his gun into ready position.

Tao sent a bullet through Yong's heart. He had no choice.

Yong crumpled to the ground, and blood pooled around his midsection. He was gone in a few seconds.

Ming stood motionless, staring at Yong's body.

"Ming, surely you understand. This is for our survival."

"I-I understand."

"Then we must hurry. Someone may come if they heard my shot."

Sixty seconds later, Ming blew a hole in the building.

Tao took the grenade launcher from Ming's hands. "Go quickly and locate the position of the BSL-4 lab. I'll watch for any intruders."

Ming hesitated.

Tao needed to satisfy Ming's concerns immediately, or his reluctance could get them all killed.

He handed Ming his QBZ-95 assault rifle. "Hurry, Ming. I need to know that lab location as much as you do."

Ming looked at the powerful rifle and smiled. He grabbed it and sprinted toward the gash in the side of the building.

***

The crack of a rifle had drawn Baker toward the sound. As he crept through trees toward the east side of the building, an explosion a hundred meters ahead shook the ground. Lights in the front of the building, near the lobby, went out.

Baker studied the area near the explosion and then called Pierce.

"Baker, is that you?"

The voice sounded tinny and distant.

"It's me. Is everything okay in the lab?"

To Baker, it sounded like there was chaos in the lab. Ryan was calling for Meiling. Then his message changed. "Meiling is unconscious."

Pierce spoke again. "I'm still suited up, so I'm talking through my radio into my phone. Whatever that explosion was shook everything in here, and it went dark. Some equipment stopped working, but the backup generator kicked on, and we're resetting everything that needs it. Should be okay in here in a couple of minutes. Could you see what happened?"

"It looked like somebody shot an RPG into the lobby area of the lab."

"Then they'll be trying to get inside. Stop them, Baker. I've got to go and check on Meiling." Pierce dropped off the call.

Baker closed his cell.

A crunching sound came from behind, and Baker whirled toward it.

"Baker, it's Rafe. Looks like the bad dudes are up ahead."

Baker turned around again.

A light flashed through the trees ahead.

He dove to the ground.

A boom slammed his head like a hammer blow.

Rafe cried out behind him.

This wasn't good. The CCP goons had gotten off another RPG round. It sounded like an anti-personnel warhead, the kind that were loaded with ball bearings.

After he regained his bearings, Baker turned around to check on Rafe.

Rafe sat on the ground behind a large tree, wrapping tape around his right thigh.

"Did you get hit, Rafe?"

"Yeah." He finished wrapping and shoved the tape into his coat pocket.

"How bad is it?"

"I was lucky. A ball bearing clipped this tree. Came right on through and took a chunk out of the side of my leg. It hurt like heck, but it isn't deep, so I slapped some QuikClot on it, taped it tight, and I'm good to go. How about you?"

"I'm fine, but the news isn't good. These guys have RPGs. I think they shot an anti-tank round into the lobby to gain access, and they shot an anti-personnel warhead at us. There's chaos in the lab, but I don't think they incurred any serious damage."

He blew out a sharp sigh. "I don't know how many CCP goons are here, but we've got to put them on the defensive now, or things will go south in a hurry."

Chapter 19

January 5, 10:30 p.m., less than three hours left for Ryan

Meiling awoke with a start. There had been a loud explosion. Now she heard gunfire coming from outside the lab.

She studied Ryan for a few seconds. He seemed nauseated and disoriented.

It was a strong indication that they needed to raise his probe level, and that required more of her probe-rich blood.

"Robert, Ryan still is not overcoming his viral load. He needs more of my blood."

The intense look in Pierce's eyes did not encourage Meiling. "I can't give Ryan any blood yet. The lab lost power. The generator kicked in, but I've got to check all the equipment to make sure nothing was reset to its default settings. And **you** can't give Ryan any blood either, not yet. Let's re-evaluate at eleven o'clock."

They were cutting things too closely for Ryan's sake. Every step of the way, the virus had been two steps ahead of their predicted schedule. What if it was breaking through his blood-brain barrier right now?

"Make sure everything is set for the blood draw and the transfusion, Robert. We have been chasing this virus from behind ever since Ryan was infected. It is time for us to take the lead."

A half-hour later, Dr. Pierce checked Ryan's IV meter. Thankfully, it was still working properly.

"Let's prepare you for drawing another half pint of blood, Meiling."

By 11:10 p.m., Pierce had drawn a half pint of Meiling's blood. The draw had left her lightheaded and struggling against losing consciousness. She needed to be alert for the critical minutes soon coming in the battle against Ryan's infection.

The battle outside had been relatively quiet for a while.

A loud boom shook her bed and raised her level of consciousness. The lights flickered again but remained on.

Meiling strained to talk to Pierce, to ask if everything was okay, but her tongue was too heavy to move. She tried to call him, but her tongue wouldn't cooperate.

Now her vision grew fuzzy and gray, and then the gray faded to black.

***

Baker's phone sounded the ringtone he had set for his team members.

"Baker here."

"This is Vance. Randy and I are at the southwest corner of the building. We think that we have them in a crossfire between you two and us."

"I believe you're right," Baker said. We're not in each other's line of fire, so shoot as much as needed to keep them pinned down."

"They're probably getting a little desperate about now."

"Yeah," Baker said. "And that worries me. They already shot off one HEAT round. They could take us both out if they have a couple more of those anti-tank rounds. We need to keep our positions hidden or disguised just in case."

"Right. We'll move after we shoot, but we'll keep you out of our shooting angle when—watch out, Baker! Weapon pointed your way."

"Down, Rafe!" Baker dove behind the nearest tree, and Rafe landed beside him.

Baker had instinctively covered his eyes with his hands. The light came through anyway, and the radiation burned the exposed part of the back of his neck.

Trees fifty or sixty feet behind them burst into flames and lit the night.

He looked at Rafe lying beside him.

Rafe wasn't moving. But now he shook his head as if trying to shake off a stunning blow.

"Rafe, are you okay?"

"Give me a second, and I will be. What happened, Baker?"

"I think they shot an HEDP at us?"

"A what?"

"A high-explosive, dual-purpose warhead. They designed them to be a compromise between armor penetration and killing dudes like us. But it hit about sixty or seventy feet behind us, just outside the injury radius for that round."

"Bro, we can't let them shoot another one of those rounds."

Baker raised his head and looked toward their enemy's position. "Those burning trees are lighting up the area like a Friday night football game."

"That means they can see us as well as we can see them," Rafer said.

"Then we need to keep them pinned down. On three, by my count. Ready. One, two, three."

The two raised their rifles and rose to a kneeling position. The enemy was visible. One man.

Baker began firing bursts in automatic mode.

Rafe sprayed his entire magazine in a long, loud staccato of cracks. "He went down."

More rifle volleys came from the far corner of the building.

"Sounds like Randy and Vance are getting in on it, too," Baker said.

"Yeah. The other dude just went down." Rafer rose to his feet.

"Be careful, Rafe."

"I'm being careful. All of them are down. I see no movement."

Baker stood. "I'm calling Vance to let him know we're moving in."

He called Vance, who quickly acknowledged.

"Rafe, let's check them out, but make sure nobody's playing possum."

Five minutes later, Baker's team of four had verified that the CCP goons were dead and that there had been three of them. Apparently, they had killed one of their own. And they had another HEDP which they had not been able to fire because Baker's team had pinned them down.

"I'll let Pierce know." Baker pulled out his phone and hit Dr. Pierce's entry on his call list.

"This is Robert. Are you all okay? It sounded like World War III out there."

"War's over," Baker said. "The CCP dudes all got a one-way trip to Hades. Actually, I'm not their judge, but atheistic communism does not save anybody. Last time I read my Bible, it still said that Jesus is the only way."

"Did we have any casualties?" Robert asked.

"No. Rafe got his leg creased. That last round was pretty hot. The back of my neck got a little sunburned. We're gonna enter your lobby through that new door you have, courtesy of the CCP. We'll rest up there and doctor ourselves up a bit."

"The key to the vending machine is under the floor mat behind the counter. Help yourselves," Robert said. "We can't come out until we're all decontaminated. I don't know when that will be. We're waiting on Ryan to respond to Meiling's therapy."

Like a pack of howling coyotes, sirens sounded in the distance. "I don't know when we'll be available to meet you," Baker said. "Evidently, some farmer, a mile or so away, heard our little war and called the police. It sounds like they sent the whole department."

"Whatever you tell them to extricate yourselves, you can mention me, but don't mention Meiling."

"I understand. Who's Meiling?"

***

Meiling awoke, but her entire body felt like her leg when it had gone to sleep from having its circulation cut off.

"Robert?" She could talk again with a little effort.

He turned toward her. "So you decided to wake up. I'll bet you need some more orange juice."

"How is Ryan doing?"

"It's too soon to see any impacts from your probe-rich blood. But remember, he's a probe factory, too, even if his factory isn't running as efficiently as yours. Now for some orange juice." Robert handed her a bottle of juice with a straw in it.

After she had taken several swallows, Meiling sat up. The room seemed to rock for a second or two, then it stabilized.

She might be weak and tired for a while, but she would soon be back to full strength. Ryan, on the other hand ...

Robert moved a chair from the workbench to her bedside and sat.

"Ryan has not been doing well since 10:30 p.m., and I think he has been asleep for at least the last half hour," Meiling said. "I do not think he even heard that big explosion that came near the end of the war. Do you think the virus has gotten into his central nervous system?"

113

"I don't think so. But there's so much we don't know about Nipah. And his case is atypical."

The familiar nauseating knot had formed again in Meiling's gut. "What do you think we should do?"

"We watch, we wait, and we pray."

That was not what Meiling wanted to hear.

It was nearly midnight.

Only an hour left.

Chapter 20

January 6, 2:00 a.m., Dr. Pierce's BSL-4 lab

Meiling collapsed on the edge of her bed. The continuous stress of the past week had worn her down.

Baker and his men had reported in. There was no sign of any further threats.

Ryan was now sleeping peacefully. That was a good sign.

She stretched out on her hospital bed and quickly drifted off.

She awoke, yawned, and checked the time. 6:00 a.m. She had slept for four hours.

Ryan sat up on the edge of his bed. "I'm hungry. But first, I want a big mug of coffee with a little cream and no sugar."

That was a very good sign.

Robert gave Meiling thumbs up with his green-gloved thumbs. "I can arrange for the coffee to be brought in."

Ryan returned Robert's thumbs up when he mentioned coffee.

Meiling sat on the bed beside Ryan and took his free hand. "You had us a bit worried when you went to sleep on us."

"I felt a little sick, but mostly just tired. I must have slept for several hours." He paused. "So, what's the verdict?"

Meiling cradled his hand in hers. "The jury is—how do you say it in America—still out? We still need to verify a couple of things, and then you and I need our probe factories shut down."

"I hope you're talking about verifying that I'm over the Nipah Virus."

"I am. We will draw some blood and check it here in the lab for NiV. If the killer probe has done its job, we'll arrange for an MRI. Robert says there is a local imaging center in Louisville, a few miles away. They have agreed to do it provided we thoroughly decontaminate you and assure them that you cannot shed enough virus to make anyone sick."

"An MRI? I didn't hurt my head while I was asleep, did I?"

"No. But we need to be sure that no **zombies** hurt your head. You know, that blood-brain-barrier thing."

"Suppose some got through and—"

"We will not go there, Ryan. I do not think you could be feeling this good if the disease progressed that far."

"Then what? Am I good to go if the MRI doesn't show anything?"

"Almost. Finally, you and I get to take naps in our hospital beds while Robert turns off the probe factories in our bodies. It will take a few hours for a couple of IVs each."

"Meiling, I've been sleeping for hours. I don't need a nap. I need ..." Ryan's eyes focused on a spot a little south of Meiling's nose.

She couldn't stifle the gasp his look triggered or her smile that followed.

The airlock light came on, and air blew in after Robert opened the door. He retrieved a large mug from the floor of the airlock, but Meiling stole it from his hands.

Coffee mug in hand, she sauntered back to Ryan. "If you promise to be good today, you can have this coffee."

"And who's the judge of my goodness?"

"Your doctor, me." Meiling handed him the coffee.

"I didn't make any promises."

"But I did. If you do not behave, I can put something in your IV that does more than just stop your killer probe factory. I can make your next twenty-four hours absolutely miserable."

"Okay. Okay. I promise."

Robert cleared his throat. It wasn't loud, but it sounded like a military officer calling the room to attention.

Meiling's cheeks grew warm as she realized she had been flirting with Ryan like a teenager. As much as she enjoyed it, that behavior had no business inside a BSL-4 facility.

"You do realize, don't you, Meiling, that you have created an effective therapeutic for the Nipah Virus?" Robert had rescued her by changing the subject.

He pointed toward the container that had held the probe's mRNA nanoparticles. "What do you plan to do with it?"

"It is not just mine, Robert. Without you and your lab, this therapy would never have come into existence. So, I ask you, what should **we** do with our therapeutic for the Nipah virus?"

"**Our** therapeutic? You are being very gracious, Meiling." Robert stroked his beard for a few seconds. "I think we should make a patent request and then, under contract, give the therapeutic and instructions for making it to a small, competent pharmaceutical company that we trust. Since they would have minimal R&D costs and we own the patent, we'll allow them to sell the injection reasonably so every third-world country can quickly stamp out any Nipah outbreaks. That should neutralize the CCP's bioweapon, and it ought to really tick them off."

"Tick them off?"

"It's an American expression for make them angry."

Meiling nodded. "The PLA still has some work to modify their NiV to fully weaponize it. But what if they realize what we have done here and decide to release the current version of NiV immediately before we can prepare for a pandemic?"

"We would have enough evidence to try them in the news media and to convict them in front of the entire world if they attempted that."

"But, Robert, is that enough of a threat to stop them from releasing a natural Nipah Virus now?"

"Good point. But remember, if it's not weaponized, it won't transmit very well." He paused. "Here's what I can do to ameliorate this situation. I'll train my staff here—hire some more if needed—and we'll keep producing the killer probe nanoparticles as fast as I can."

"What about storing them? The COVID-19 vaccine nanoparticles had to be stored at extremely low temperatures, and that created problems for vaccine distribution."

Robert stroked his beard two or three times. "Researchers at Stanford have been working on mRNA vaccines containing nanoparticles that can be stored at room temperature. Even if I can't take advantage of their work, we'll find a way to store our Nipah killer and then ask the government for a grant to optimize the storage and to build up a supply for the U.S. to be used in an emergency. We can probably do all that before the CCP or PLA can weaponize their virus for mass infection and before they can produce enough to be a threat."

"You are proposing a defensive deterrent?" Meiling said. "I guess this is not like the Cold War, where America had powerful offensive weapons for deterrents. Maybe a strong defensive deterrent will work in this new world of government-run bioterrorism. But can such a defensive tactic strike terror in the hearts of the CCP so that they will not release their biowarfare weapons?"

Robert sighed. "I guess that is the salient question."

"Yes," Meiling said. "Simply stated, the question is, how do you deter a biowarfare threat?"

"Simple," Ryan said.

Meiling and Robert turned their heads toward Ryan.

"Simple?" Meiling cocked her head.

"Yeah. You first need a strong president. He or she must look the leader of the CCP in the eye, tell them that we will assume the CCP and their bioweapons program caused the next pandemic and that they will get a nuclear response they won't survive. Then we see who blinks first. Just like the Cold War."

He paused.

"Now, when do I get that MRI?"

Meiling scanned him from head to foot. "After we decontaminate you."

"Decontaminate? What does that entail?" Ryan's focus darted back and forth between Meiling and Robert.

Meiling gave him the cheesiest smirk she could produce. "First, we remove all your clothes and put them in a laundry bin for decontamination. Then we scrub you in the shower for at least three minutes with a special soap. We dry you off, and then you put on clean clothes."

"Who's **we**?"

"Robert and me."

"Meiling, I can't do that."

"Why not? I'm just your doctor."

"Yeah, right. Besides, I didn't bring any other clothes."

"I'll get them for you. I've heard you can buy anything you need at a Super Walmart."

Chapter 21

January 7, The next day, 45,000 feet above Western Colorado

Meiling sat beside Ryan on a small couch, the nearest seat to the cockpit of Baker's Gulfstream. They were headed back to Redmond. Sometime after they got there, all they had accomplished at Pierce's lab and the joy it brought Meiling would be nullified once Ryan learned the truth about her.

Meiling's life since becoming a follower of Jesus was nothing but a series of failures and bad choices. Even her decision to take the fellowship at Wuhan was—what had the Apostle Paul called it—something done out of selfish ambition?

While at Wuhan, she couldn't, rather wouldn't, attend church because of the damage it could do to her career. Though she never committed any immoral acts with men, the attention a woman like her drew in an organization like the WIV brought sexual harassment to Meiling. Instead of blunt refusals to their overtures, she often led these men on for a while to turn their attention into opportunities to accomplish her own goals. This included lying and deception that were done out of selfish ambition.

Worst of all, when someone suspected she was a secret Christian and the police questioned her, she denied Jesus rather than risk her position and possible punishment.

After recalling her failures, shame welled deep inside Meiling.

Was this the kind of woman a man like Ryan deserved? Would he even want her if he knew?

Why hadn't she raised this issue in her own mind before now? Probably because there was danger and there were other issues that demanded immediate attention, or someone might die.

Ryan reached for her hand.

She moved it and clasped her hands.

Ryan's face held a look of suspicion. "You're sure quiet. So much happened in the last two days that there is a lot to reflect on. But we survived, Meiling, thanks in a large part to you. Now we have a future to look forward to and plans to make."

It was time. Meiling needed to summon the courage to tell Ryan the truth. She could never live up to his standards. Her past proved that. Ryan deserved better.

"Ryan, I know that contacting you as I did will likely mean that you must change your life. You cannot go back to your job and the exposure that television broadcasting gives you. And you may have to hide like I will have to do."

"We're two people who both need to hide from the same people for the same reasons." He smiled warmly. "Sounds like we should hide together."

Meiling scooted an inch or two away from Ryan.

His eyes said he noticed.

"There are reasons why we should not."

Ryan dropped his gaze to the floor of the airplane. "I don't understand, Meiling."

She didn't reply.

"You can't make a statement like that and not even explain it."

"You do not know my past, Ryan. You barely know my present. I-I am not a good person. Not good enough for someone like you ... let alone for a holy God."

"Meiling, I've never known anyone so giving, so willing to sacrifice themselves for others. You are much better than I deserve."

"That is not true. Do you want me to tell you in detail all that I have done? Things that will always be held against me."

"Always be held against you? That is not the way God deals with—"

"I am going to the lavatory." She unbuckled her seat belt and stood.

Her glance toward the lavatory revealed Baker standing near the doorway of the cockpit. Hopefully, the humming of the engines had prevented Baker from hearing their conversation. But the engines on this plane were mounted so far to the rear that it was relatively quiet near the front of the cabin where Meiling and Ryan were sitting.

Meiling hurried to the lavatory, avoiding eye contact with Baker.

***

Baker couldn't believe what he had heard. What was it Dr. Pierce had told him? Those two are a perfect match, even their blood types?

Ryan looked like George Foreman in his prime had just punched Ryan in his solar plexus.

If Baker talked to Ryan now, it would be loud enough that Meiling might hear in the lavatory between the two men.

He motioned toward Ryan.

Slowly he unbuckled his seat belt and approached Baker.

"Dude, what's with Meiling? Or should I ask what's with you and Meiling?"

Ryan blew out a sharp sigh. "In a nutshell ... I think Meiling doesn't understand forgiveness. And I don't even know what she thinks needs to be forgiven."

"I've got an idea. Take your seat, bro, before she comes out."

"This is important, Baker. You'd better let me in on whatever it is you're doing."

"I'll give you a clue. One word. Munchkin."

"Shauna?"

Baker nodded and pointed toward a seat farther back in the cabin than where Ryan had been sitting with Meiling.

He followed Baker's advice and walked back to the seat.

When Meiling emerged from the lavatory, she glanced at Baker. Her eyes were visibly red even from ten feet away.

Baker motioned her his way.

She sauntered tentatively to the front of the cabin. "You are supposed to be in the pilot's seat."

"Not to worry. The autopilot on a Gulfstream 550 is solid as a rock. Regardless, I'm not supposed to leave the cockpit."

"That is good to know. Why did you want to see me?"

"We'll be landing in about forty minutes. My wife, Shauna, and our twins will be there. I'd like to introduce you to her. You two have a lot in common."

Why had he added that last sentence? A lot in common—it wasn't exactly true. In fact, it was because of their differences that he wanted them to talk. There probably wasn't a lot the two women had in common—a beautiful, Asian, world-class medical researcher and a cute, tiny, African American woman with a temperament composed of equal parts honey and habanero.

On the other hand, they both had Jesus.

Baker returned to the pilot seat and dialed Shauna's number on the Gulfstream 550's iridium sat phone.

"Is that you, Runt?"

"It's me, Munchkin."

"I see you're calling from the plane. Are you on your way home? The answer had better be yes."

"We're a little more than a half-hour out. Could you do me a big favor and be at the airport jet center when we arrive? Bring the girls with you."

"Me grant you a favor? Remember, the next time you ask if you can go flying off to Colorado in the middle of the night, the answer's no." Her voice broke on the last two words. "The girls and I need you, Baker. You are a veteran, an ex-soldier. Your combat days are over. Do you hear?"

"Yes, sir. Loud and clear."

"I'll be at the jet center with the girls when you land."

"Sweetheart, I'm going to introduce you to Meiling. She needs to talk to you."

"Why does a Chinese medical researcher need to talk to me?"

"I think she has a problem with forgiveness."

"I see. Mr. Baker, if you keep flying off into war zones, you might have a problem with forgiveness too."

***

Meiling watched with curiosity as a petite African American woman approached, dodging shallow puddles on the tarmac from recent rain. Shauna had what appeared to be three-year-old twin girls hanging onto her hands.

Baker strode Meiling's way and stopped beside her as the very pretty woman with the twins arrived.

The girls ran to Baker, and each grabbed a leg to hug.

Shauna's arms circled his neck. She spoke too softly for Meiling to hear.

Shauna stepped back from Baker, and he hooked an arm around her waist. "Meiling, this is my wife, Shauna, and my daughters, Deborah and Sarah. Shauna, this is Meiling, whom you probably have heard a lot about in the news."

"It's good to finally meet you, Meiling. Now, Rad, would you please take the girls for a few minutes. They've nearly worn me out."

"Sure, Munchkin. Girls …" He scooped up one in each arm and ambled away toward Ryan, who stood at a distance watching the scene before him unfold.

Shauna appeared to be studying Meiling's face.

Hopefully, her hurt and disappointment did not show.

"Meiling, how did things go in Colorado?"

"Very well. We were able to keep Ryan from getting sick with the deadly Nipah Virus, and we believe we created a cure for Nipah."

"Sounds like the trip was successful, but I was thinking more about your and Ryan's relationship. We have been praying for a long time for Ryan to find someone."

How did she know about that? Baker must have said something. Regardless, it wasn't a subject to discuss with a stranger, even if Baker thought there was some benefit from Meiling talking with his wife.

Maybe Meiling should be blunt. Just dump it all on Shauna. That might stop this painful discussion about a sensitive subject before it became a torture chamber.

"Shauna, Ryan is an authentic Jesus follower. He knows God's word and defends it as an apologist. But a person like me—I'm not worthy of someone like him."

Shauna squinted as in disbelief. "I don't see how you can think that. You saved his life, and if I heard the story correctly, he saved yours."

"You need to hear my version of the story. Two years ago, the CCP offered me an extremely attractive fellowship to lure me to the Wuhan lab. It is not a good place for Christians. I compromised my faith too many times to count while I was there. I am not worthy of a man like Ryan. I am not even worthy of the friends I have found here in America, Dr. Pierce, and your husband. To me, they are like the heroes of the faith we read about in the Bible. But I am someone who squandered their forgiveness. Does not the

Bible say something like whoever denies Jesus does not have the Father?"

"I think you took that verse a little out of context." Shauna's hands went to her hips. "What terrible thing did you do that God won't forgive?"

"Someone at the lab told the CCP that I was a Christian. The military police came and questioned me and asked if I believed in Jesus. I said no. I told them I could never believe in myths and, furthermore—"

"Whooooa, girl. This isn't people's forgiveness we're talking about. People may give forgiveness, take it back, and give it again, but that's not how it works with God. You need to learn how wide, and long, and high, and deep Jesus' love for you is."

"I have heard about that but—"

"Well, you're gonna hear it again." Shauna moved beside Meiling, pulled out her cell, and opened a Bible app. "So you believe that you denied your faith. Out of fear, maybe you did say those words. Of course, that was wrong, but there are worse sinners than you. Take the Apostle Paul. He had innocent Christians put to death. He was a murderer. Later, he called himself the chief of sinners because of what he had done. But did he let that stop him?"

"I know you are going to say that he did not."

"But why am I gonna say that?"

Meiling didn't reply.

"First, I'm saying it because the Apostle Peter did the same exact thing you did, and he did it while standing in Jesus' presence." She paused.

"Secondly, I'm saying it because the Apostle Paul wrote these words for us all." She glanced down at the cell phone's display. "He said, 'If God is for us, who can be against us?' It doesn't even matter who accuses us of doing wrong. It doesn't matter because God is the only one who can justify us. If that's true, it doesn't matter who tries to condemn us, and it doesn't matter if we try to condemn ourselves. We can't condemn ourselves, Meiling. Not if God has justified us. He is the only one who can justify."

Shauna paused.

Was Shauna done? Why did she stop after her statement about being justified? Justification was a legal act that gave a person good standing and kept them from being punished. But what about the cries of a human heart? What about Meiling's desire to know and feel that she was loved and accepted?

Shauna continued. "Paul asked who could separate us from the love of Jesus. He gave a long, complete answer, a list that left out nothing—not death and not life, angels or demons, things in the present or the future, no power that exists, not the dimensions of space, nor anything else in His entire creation. Nothing can ever separate us from God's love in Jesus Christ. Nothing."

The words weren't entirely new to Meiling, but the reality of them, as they applied to her life, had just come into clearer focus.

Shauna studied her face for a moment. "I think maybe you're getting it. That list doesn't leave out anything. Not even an endangered young woman who lied out of fear while being interrogated by an authority that could throw her in prison and torture her."

Shauna paused. "Have you asked to be forgiven?"

Meiling nodded.

"Good. You are free to walk in fellowship with God, Meiling. One day you will be with Him in heaven because you have been forgiven. Your lies are as if they had never been spoken. As far as the east is from the west, they were removed from you. Girl, that's what it means to be forgiven. It's for freedom that Jesus set us free."

Again, Meiling didn't reply. How could she? There was no defense for the conclusions she had drawn. But realizing that still did not make her feel any better.

"One more thing. Can you name even one thing you've ever done that Jesus' sacrifice wasn't good enough to cover, something that his blood couldn't wash clean?"

"I—I …."

"Come on, Meiling. Surely you can name one terrible thing you did that Jesus couldn't take care of." Shauna paused.

"Meiling, you're not saying anything. Talk to me … name it, girl. Just one thing."

The reality came like an explosion of light, lighting every part of Meiling and cleansing her at the same time. How could she keep a sin from her past between her and God when God said it was gone, dealt with, paid for?

What did Jesus say when he died?

It is finished.

Jesus' words spoken from the cross seemed to roll through her heart and mind like the thundering jet now accelerating down the runway.

What had Pastor Lin told Meiling that those words meant? Literally, it is finished. But to a prisoner, they said that the debt had been paid. The penalty for her crime against God had been paid too … by Jesus.

Meiling wiped her cheeks and pulled Shauna close to her. "Thank you. I did not realize that it was Jesus, not me, that I was hurting and putting down by telling Him that He had not done enough, that He was not good enough. I will not do that to Him anymore nor to myself."

"It also hurts those around you when you do that. Now, what are you going to do about Ryan Adams?"

Meiling leaned back to see Shauna's face. "I'm going to tell him I was just released from a mental institution and see if he will forgive me."

Shauna giggled and her eyes danced. But they quickly reverted to the intensity of the previous five minutes.

"Just tell him the truth. And the truth is, girl, you didn't know the truth. You only **thought** you did."

"I know now, and I'll tell him."

"It's time for you to live free, Meiling, because you **are** free. And this is how it feels to be free."

Chapter 22

January 7, Private Jet Center, Redmond Municipal Airport

Meiling hurried across the tarmac to a big Jeep SUV where Ryan and Baker stood, each holding a girl in one arm.

As she approached, Ryan set the girl down. His face displayed the taut expression it held on the plane when she told him they had no future together.

Baker now held both the twins. "If you two want to hang out here and talk, I'll take Sarah and Deborah over to my Trackhawk and get them ready for the ride home."

Ryan nodded. "Thanks."

Baker ambled away with his girls.

Shauna joined him.

It was time for Meiling's plea, and she prayed Ryan would understand. She looked up into his eyes. "I'm insane ... I mean I was, but I'm not anymore."

"Being wrong is not insanity, Meiling."

"If you are wrong about God, it is."

"If you have something to say, please, just tell me."

"I did something. I did what Peter did ... but I didn't do what Paul did, rather what Saul did."

"I just want to know what Meiling is going to do."

"I'm going to do what Shauna said. Live free because I am free."

"That sounds like good advice."

"Yes, it does because I'm free to plan a future that includes you, Ryan Adams, if you'll forgive me."

"How could I not forgive the woman who risked her life to save mine?" Ryan took a single step toward her.

Meiling gave in to her overflowing joy and the freedom to express it.

She threw herself into Ryan's waiting arms and allowed the last vestiges of her torment to flow away in the tears that streamed down her cheeks and down Ryan's neck.

An hour later, Baker delivered Ryan and Meiling to Ryan's SUV, which was still parked along the forest service road near Skeleton Cave.

The date written on the rear window said the SUV would be towed in another day if the vehicle were not moved.

Ryan slipped into the driver's seat. The vehicle started and ran smoothly. "At least the cold weather didn't break my engine block."

Meiling walked around his SUV and saw no damage.

"Looks like you two are good to go here," Baker said. "I'm gonna head back to my family before Munchkin turns from honey to habanero. You know how she can be." He met Ryan's gaze, then Meiling's. "I mean this—if you need my help, I'm available. And if you cook up some scheme that needs an airplane, my birds are available. See you two later."

How could they pay Baker for flying his Gulfstream? How could he keep ferrying Meiling around when it likely cost him more than a thousand dollars per hour just to fly it, and that didn't even include maintenance and other costs? She added compensating Baker to her growing list of concerns she and Ryan needed to tend to as they mapped out their future.

She climbed into the passenger seat beside Ryan.

He glanced her way then turned and focused on some distant spot down the road or perhaps somewhere in the distant future.

He sighed and turned to face her. "You have a lot of plans to make, Meiling."

"No. **We** have a lot of plans to make."

"Well, let's drive back to my house and make them over a pot of coffee or Seattle tea." He took her hand, lifted it to his lips, and kissed it.

Her first kiss from Ryan Adams—right on the knuckle of her index finger. He'd had something else in mind after he recovered from the virus while they were in Robert's lab.

But Meiling could wait ... for a little while. "It's still rather cold here, though the rain seems to have melted much of the snow. Tea sounds wonderful."

A few minutes later, Ryan had turned up the heat in his house, built a roaring fire in the fireplace, and handed Meiling a cup of hot water with a tea bag in it.

Ryan placed two dining chairs in front of the fire.

Meiling left the tea bag in her cup to let the tea brew as strongly as it could while she slowly sipped it. As the fire and tea warmed her and the caffeine added its boost, the future and what it would require came into focus.

"Ryan, you've got to make some radical life changes. I hope that's okay with you."

"I'm just a local TV meteorologist. What changes are you talking about?"

"You were involved with me in a scheme that upset the CCP's plan for eventual world domination. Their biowarfare weapons are part of their unrestricted warfare tactic. By now, you and I have been in the news internationally. It would not be wise for you to continue in your highly visible job as a TV meteorologist. The CCP never forget nor forgive what they consider to be treachery. They know where you are and will pay you and me and Dr. Pierce for what we have done. They will be a continual threat for the rest of our lives ... or theirs."

"What about you, Meiling? What did you do with that Form I-589, Application for Asylum, that Pierce downloaded for you before we left?"

"It is in my purse. First, we should decide which USCIS office I should submit it to. But before I apply for asylum, I must squelch the media's story that I was transporting a dangerous virus."

"In reality, you were transporting just the opposite, information that could kill dangerous viruses." His chuckle morphed into a smile that quickly faded. "And you need somewhere to hide. Somewhere that's safe."

"You need a place to hide too. The CCP knows you, and they know you have been with me. They will assume you know all my secrets."

"I wish I did." He grinned at her and scanned her from head to foot.

"You are impossible. This is serious. When they come again, it will be to kill both of us.

"Maybe Pierce, too," Ryan said.

She sipped her tea and stared into the fire. "Yes, Pierce too."

"Meiling, he made it clear that he hates the evil being done in the PLA labs and the Wuhan Institute of Virology. He hates it as much as we do."

Meiling looked up at Ryan. "The members of the CCP running the biowarfare part of their unrestricted warfare program are among the evilest people on the planet."

"And because the West, especially America, does not retaliate—we do absolutely nothing—intelligence shows that the CCP has more biowarfare weapons ready to deploy. And they have new ones in development. To stop all this, we must hold the CCP accountable."

Her cheeks had grown warm from the fire, but thoughts of what the CCP and PLA were doing made her anger flash hot. "These people are doing what Satan does. He kills, steals, and destroys. I wish I could destroy all their research and their lab too."

Ryan caught her gaze, including the laser-like intensity of those almond-shaped eyes. "Meiling, aren't you the most qualified person on this planet to do just that?"

"What are you saying, Ryan?"

He laid a hand on her shoulder. "Only that if you feel strongly about holding them accountable and stopping the biowarfare work of the CCP and PLA, you should determine if God is calling you to fight that battle."

She moved closer and laid her head on his shoulder. "If so, I would need a strong Jesus follower at my side to advise me, especially to advise me spiritually." She raised her head and peered into his eyes. "And I would need another scientist to help me formulate and sanity check our plans. I would also have to recruit an accomplice from the workers at the lab in Wuhan."

"In Wuhan? Is that even possible?"

"Yes." She raised her head and looked into his eyes. "There are many Chinese, even in the Wuhan lab, who despise the CCP and the way it has butchered people in its organ-harvesting program, the way it has imprisoned innocent people, and its attempted genocide on others. And they despise the twenty-four-hour surveillance of everything they say and do."

"Is that a strong enough motive to risk their lives?"

"If they trust us to tell the truth to the world, someone there will give us the intelligence information we need to expose the CCP, the PLA, and their biowarfare plans. If we are careful, perhaps we can destroy some of their research or neutralize it with our own research once we understand what they are creating. I am certain that I can find one or more of these brave Chinese people. But it might be dangerous for us to probe for them."

"Well, there you have it—"

"No, Ryan. That is not all. Remember, all of us would be putting our lives at risk, maybe even Baker, if he continues to help us. You have already seen what these people will do. And the danger would likely last for the rest of our lives. It would impact the lives of our childr—I mean, if we were to ... uh ..."

"I know what you mean, Meiling. If you're ready for this war against Satan and his CCP minions, there's no one else I'd rather have at my side than you." He grinned. "And it's a spiritually healthy thing for children to see their parents dedicated to fighting for what's good and right, no matter how high the stakes."

Meiling laid her head on his shoulder again and spoke softly. "Then we should ask Robert if he will join us."

Ryan chuckled. It soon morphed into belly-shaking laughter.

Meiling leaned away from him. "Ryan, that wasn't meant to be funny."

"I know. But after all Robert has seen, I wouldn't want to be the person who tried to stop him."

"You are right." They both stood, and Meiling pulled him into a warm embrace. "Then we should go invite Dr. Robert Pierce to join us."

He returned her warm hug with one of his own. "Yes. It's time for us to declare war on the CCP's biological weapons program." Ryan kissed her forehead.

He was getting better. Only about six inches off the target.

"As we declare this war, maybe God will give us opportunities to shine His light into a very dark and blind nation in—what shall we call this, Ryan—our war *against the darkness*?"

The end ... of the beginning ...

135

Acknowledgments

Thanks to my wife, Babe, for her many suggestions for making *Facing the Darkness* a better story and for listening to me read her the story multiple times to catch the plot holes and the logical errors.

Thanks to my wife, Babe, for her many suggestions for making *Facing the Darkness* a better story and for listening to me read her the story several times to catch the plot holes and the logical errors.

Thank you again, Samantha Fury, for capturing the essence of the story in the cover design—a brave young woman facing her fears and the evil that hides in the darkness to destroy all that is good.

Thank you, Gail Ostheller, for proofing *Facing the Darkness* to catch errors that my aging eyes seem to miss more frequently these days.

Thanks to The Epoch Times and NTD News for their excellent coverage of China news, without which this series could not have been written with any degree of realism.

And, of course, I thank my Heavenly Father for leaving me enough words and wits to finish another novel.

Author's Notes

Facing the Darkness is the prequel in the *Against the Darkness Series*, a story about a brilliant, young Chinese virologist, Dr. Meiling Chen, who declares a personal war against the CCP's biowarfare program and flees to the U.S. where she forms a private sector team to counter China's biowarfare weapons. (*Can you say COVID-19?*)

If you travel to Southeast Asia, beware of any Nipah cases in the area. This rare but deadly virus has only produced about seven hundred human cases in the past twenty years, but in the real world there is no Dr. Meiling Chen with the skills to cure you. However, Nipah is an RNA virus. So, in theory, the methods of reducing viral load used in my story seem like a good approach. They worked well for my wife and me when we had COVID, which is also caused by an RNA virus.

The character, Dr. Meiling Chen, MD, Ph.D., was patterned somewhat after a real-life heroine, Dr. Li-Meng Yan, an MD, Ph.D. and a Post-doctoral Fellow in the School of Public Health at the University of Hong Kong. Despite the media's malicious mockery, she continued to tell us the truth about COVID-19 and the Communist Chinese Party's guilt and their deceptive methods used to disguise their international bioweapons research. Dr. Yan had professional and insider knowledge, knowledge that was completely lacking in the mainstream media who taunted and ridiculed her. Boo! Hiss!

She escaped—did you get that, ***escaped?***—from Hong Kong in April of 2020 after exposing the CCP's role in COVID-19 which forced the CCP to alter their strategy on the origin of the virus. The truth that is slowly being acknowledged today has vindicated her revelation of China's culpability that she began exposing in January 2020. Do not believe what is posted about her on Wikipedia. Just sayin' ...

Facing the Darkness is my first attempt at something like a medical thriller. Nearly two years of research went into that effort. I hope I got the medical aspects right and still entertained you.

If you enjoyed *Facing the Darkness*, please leave a review on Amazon for this book.

https://www.amazon.com/stores/author/B00B1XMR56

This helps other readers find books they will enjoy and is a wonderful way to encourage the author. You can reach me on Facebook as H L Wegley or Harry Wegley or through my author website:

https://www.hlwegley.com

And be sure to read Chapter 1 of *The Darkness Beyond* starting on the next page.

Chapter 1 from book 2, *The Darkness Beyond:*

8:00 a.m. MDT, Dr. Pierce's guest apartment, the morning after Meiling's wedding

Meiling slid toward Ryan's side of the bed and poked his shoulder where the Nipah-infected dart had hit him two months ago. "Sweetheart, wake up. You need to answer your phone."

Ryan's eyes popped open. "Answer my phone? Why? Anyone foolish enough to call us at eight o'clock the morning after our wedding deserves to be ignored."

"But it must be important, or they would have waited."

"Important? Meiling, you are the most important thing in my life, not some ringtone on my sat phone."

"So now I'm a **thing**?"

"That's not what I meant."

She gave him her coy smile. "I know. But what if we were going to be attacked again by another gang of CCP goons?"

Ryan blasted out a sigh, pushed the sheet aside, and sat up on the edge of the bed. "Okay. To ease the mind of my beautiful bride." He picked up the call. "What do you want, nitwit?"

Meiling gasped. Ryan's speakerphone was on, but there was only silence on the other end of the line.

"Come on, nitwit. Spit it out, or I'm going to cut you off like you deserve."

He turned and looked down at Meiling lying on the bed beside him and muted the phone with his hand. "Someone on the other end just cleared their throat." He pulled his hand from the phone. "Well? What's it gonna be?"

Meiling sat up on the bed and leaned in to listen.

"Mr. Adams must have gotten up on the wrong side of the bed this morning." It was a woman's voice.

"You got that right, dufus. I just married the most beautiful woman in the world yesterday, and you have the gall to—"

"Mr. Adams, I am truly sorry for the inconvenience, but this is an important matter that cannot wait."

"Everything can wait, Ms. Who-Ever-You-Are."

"Mr. Adams, President Warrington needs to speak with you and Meiling as soon as possible, today or tomorrow morning at the latest."

"The president, you say. Well, put him on the line, if you actually can, Ms. ... uh—"

"Ms. Conroe, the president's Chief of Staff."

So Ryan was speaking to Kendall Conroe, the most powerful woman in America, alias nitwit.

Meiling placed her hand on his forehead. "Sweetheart, are you sick?" she whispered. "You don't look well."

He moved Meiling's hand and blew out a sharp sigh. "I'm sorry, Ma'am, uh ... Ms. Conroe."

"I understand. No apology is needed. But the president needs to talk to you and Meiling face-to-face as soon as possible. And you must tell no one about the meeting—not who it is with, the time, the place, nor the subject."

Meiling snuggled up to Ryan and stuck her face beside his. "Ms. Conroe, this is Meiling. We have a pilot who can fly us wherever you need us to be for a meeting late this afternoon."

"Hello, Ms. Chen—I mean Mrs. Adams. The president will slip away quietly to Camp David this afternoon at 4:00 p.m. Will that work for you?"

"That should be fine," Ryan said. "But let me talk to our pilot before I give you our ETA. What's the closest airport to Camp David?"

"It's Hagerstown Regional. After you give us your ETA, we will arrange a car to pick you up."

"There will be four of us," Meiling said.

"Four? Are you sure they all need to come?"

"Yes, Ms. Conroe," Ryan said. "That's the inner core of our team. Anything we do needs to be coordinated between the four of us."

"Before I can clear the other two for the meeting, I will need their names."

"Radley Baker and Dr. Robert Pierce," Meiling said.

"Dr. Pierce has a current Top-Secret clearance," Ryan said. "Baker had a Top-Secret SCI clearance in the military."

"Thank you. Call me at this number when you have an ETA." Ms. Conroe ended the call.

"There goes our Maui honeymoon." Meiling circled his neck with her arms and rested her head on his shoulder. "We were going to leave the day after tomorrow."

"Maybe we still can leave then. It depends on what the president wants. But right now, I need to call Baker and Pierce to let them know we're all going camping."

"Sweetheart, this camping trip could change all our lives … forever."

H.L. WEGLEY

The Darkness Beyond

Against the Darkness 2

https://www.amazon.com/stores/H.-L.-Wegley/author/B00B1XMR56

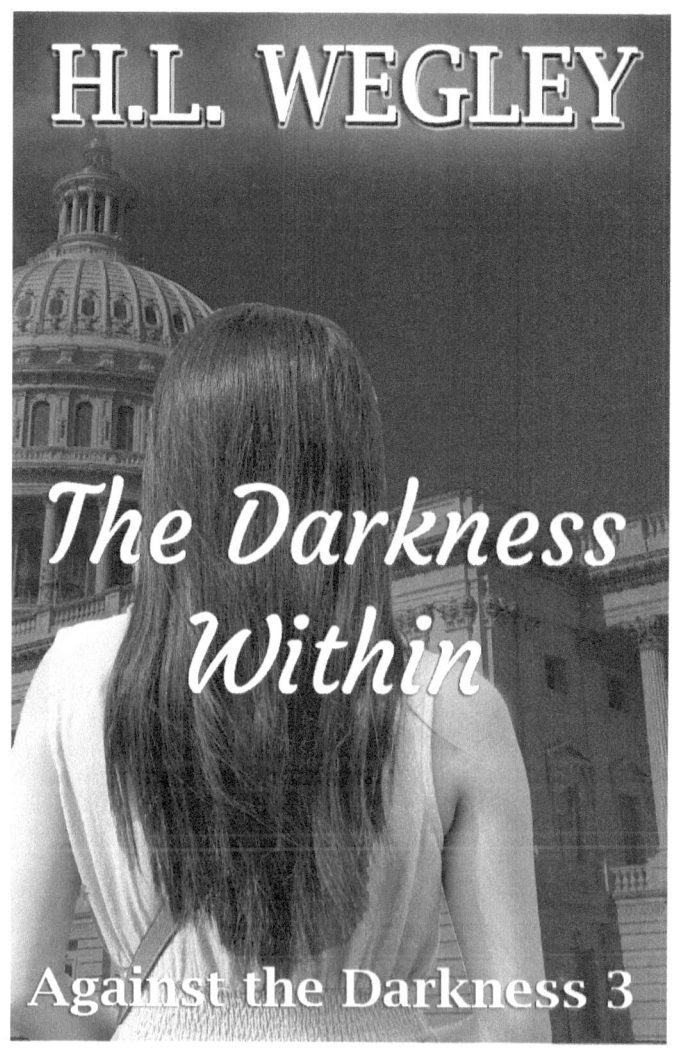

www.ingramcontent.com/pod-product-compliance
Lightning Source LLC
Chambersburg PA
CBHW050822180626
46814CB00004B/1418